An Illustrated Treasury of

GRIMM'S
FAIRY TALES

An Illustrated Treasury of

GRIMM'S
FAIRY TALES

ILLUSTRATED BY DANIELA DRESCHER

Floris Books

The illustrations in this book were hand-crafted
using watercolour paints and ink.

First published in German as *Die 100 schönsten Märchen der
Brüder Grimm* by Verlag Urachhaus, Stuttgart in 2012
This selection first published in English by Floris Books in 2013
Eighth printing 2021
© 2012 Verlag Freies Geistesleben & Urachhaus GmbH
English version © 2013 Floris Books
All rights reserved. No part of this book may be reproduced
without the prior permission of Floris Books, Edinburgh
www.florisbooks.co.uk

British Library CIP data available
ISBN 978-086315-947-3
Printed in China through Imago

Floris Books supports sustainable forest management
by printing this book on materials made from wood that
comes from responsible sources and reclaimed material

MIX
Paper from
responsible sources
FSC® C005748

Contents

1. The Princess and the Frog   7
2. The Wolf and the Seven Little Goats   13
3. Brother and Sister   18
4. Rapunzel   25
5. The Three Little Men in the Wood   31
6. Hansel and Gretel   38
7. The Fisherman and his Wife   47
8. Cinderella   56
9. Mother Holle   64
10. The Seven Ravens   69
11. Little Red Riding Hood   73
12. The Town Musicians of Bremen   77
13. Puss in Boots   82
14. Sleeping Beauty   89
15. Snow White and the Seven Dwarfs   94
16. Rumpelstiltskin   106
17. The Two Brothers   111
18. The Golden Goose   131
19. Jorinda and Jorindel   137
20. The Goose Girl   142

21. The Two Kings' Children   151

22. The Clever Little Tailor   161

23. The Four Skilful Brothers   166

24. One-Eye, Two-Eyes, Three-Eyes   173

25. The Star Money   183

26. Snow White and Rose Red   186

27. Strong Hans   196

28. The House in the Forest   205

29. The Shoemaker and the Elves   211

30. The Goose Girl at the Well   214

1

The Princess and the Frog

In olden times, there lived a King whose daughters were all beautiful, but the youngest was so very beautiful that the sun itself was astonished whenever it shone in her face. When the day was very warm, the beautiful youngest princess would go out into the forest near the castle and sit down by the side of a cool well. She would take a golden ball to throw high in the air and catch. It was her favourite toy.

One day, instead of the princess's golden ball falling back towards her hand, it went straight down the well. The well was so deep that the bottom could not be seen. She cried and cried, until, through her sobs, she heard someone saying, "What troubles you, Princess? You weep so hard, even a stone would pity you."

She looked in the direction of the voice, and saw a frog stretching its big, ugly head from the water. She said, "I am weeping for my golden ball, which has fallen into the well."

"I can help you, but what will you give me if I bring back your toy?" answered the frog.

"Whatever you want, dear frog," she said. "My clothes, my pearls and jewels, even my golden crown."

"I do not want your clothes, your pearls and jewels, nor your golden crown, but if you will love me and let me be your companion, and sit by you, and eat off your golden plate with you, and sleep in your bed – if you will promise me this, I will go down and find your golden ball."

"Oh, yes," she said, "I promise you all you wish, if you will bring me back my ball." But what she thought was *What silly things this frog says! All he does is sit in the water with the other frogs and croak. He could never be a companion to a human being!*

But the frog heard her promise, and sank deep into the well. A short while later he swam up with the golden ball in his mouth, and threw it on the grass. The princess was delighted and immediately ran off with it.

"Wait, wait," called the frog. "Take me with you. I can't run as fast as you."

The princess did not listen. She ran home and soon forgot the poor frog.

The next day, the princess was dining with the King and all the courtiers, eating from her little golden plate, when something came creeping, splish splash, splish splash, up the castle's marble staircase. There was a knock on the castle door and someone calling, "Princess, youngest Princess, open the door for me."

She ran to see who was outside, and there sat the frog. She slammed the door shut, then sat down to dinner again. The King asked, "My child, what are you so afraid of?

Is there a giant outside who wants to carry you away?"

"Ah, no," replied she, "it is not a giant, but a disgusting frog."

"What does the frog want with you?"

"Dear Father, yesterday, as I was playing in the forest, my golden ball fell into the well. The frog fetched it for me, and because he insisted, I promised him he could be my companion, but I never thought he would be able to leave the well! Now he is at the door, and wants to come in."

The frog kept knocking and calling to the princess.

The King said, "If you have made a promise, you must keep it. Go and let him in."

The princess opened the door. The frog hopped inside and followed her. He cried, "Lift me up beside you." She hesitated, until the King commanded her to do as the frog asked. Once the frog was on the chair he wanted to be on the table, and when he was on the table he said, "Now, push your little golden plate nearer to me so that we may eat together."

The frog enjoyed his food, but the princess could not eat.

Then the frog said, "Now I am tired. Carry me to your room, make your silken bed ready. We will both lie down and sleep.

The princess began to cry, for she was afraid of the cold, wet frog, who she did not like to touch, and who now wanted to sleep in her pretty, clean bed. But the King grew angry and said, "He helped you when you were in trouble. Don't be cruel to him."

So she took hold of the frog with two fingers and carried him upstairs. She put him in a corner of her room, but once she was in bed, he crept close and said, "I am tired, lift me up into bed or I will tell your father."

The princess was terribly angry. She picked up the frog and threw him with all her might against the wall. "Now, will you be quiet, horrible frog?"

But when he got up, he wasn't a frog anymore. He was a young King, with kind and beautiful eyes.

He said to the princess, "A wicked witch cast a spell on me, turning me into a frog. No one could have rescued me from the spell but you, a beautiful princess. Tomorrow, let's be married and go together to my kingdom." The princess agreed.

They went to sleep, and next morning when the sun woke them, a carriage was waiting with eight white horses. Behind stood the young King's servant, faithful Henry.

Faithful Henry had been so deeply miserable when his master was changed into a frog that he had three iron bands fastened round his heart to stop it bursting with sadness. Now he was full of joy that the spell had been broken.

When they had travelled a short way, the young King and the princess heard a cracking noise as if something had broken. The young King cried, "Henry, the carriage is breaking!"

"No, master, it is not the carriage. It is a band from my heart, which was put there in my great pain when you were a frog and imprisoned in the well."

Again, and once again, something cracked. Each time the young King thought the carriage was breaking, but it was the bands springing from faithful Henry's heart, because his master was now free and happy.

2

The Wolf and the Seven Little Goats

Once upon a time there was an old mother goat who had seven little goats. She loved her children dearly.

One day the mother goat needed to fetch some food from the forest. She called her seven little goats to come close and she said, "I have to go into the forest. Be on your guard against the wolf! If he comes in, he will eat you up. He often disguises himself, but you will know it is him because he has a rough voice and black feet."

The little goats said, "Don't worry, Mother, we will take good care of ourselves."

So the mother goat left, feeling content.

A short time later, someone knocked at the door and cried, "Open the door, dear children, your mother is here, and I have brought something back from the forest for each of you." But the little goats knew that it was the wolf's voice because it was rough.

"We will not open the door," they called back. "You are

not our mother. She has a soft, pleasant voice, and your voice is rough. You are the wolf!"

So the wolf went and bought himself a great lump of chalk, which he ate to make his voice sound soft. Then he came back, knocked at the door and cried, "Open the door, dear children, your mother is here, and I have brought something back from the forest for each of you." But he was resting his black front paws against the window, and the children saw them. They cried,

"We will not open the door! Our mother does not have black feet: you are the wolf!"

So the wolf ran to the miller and said, "Sprinkle some white flour over my feet." The miller thought to himself that the wolf must be trying to deceive someone, and he refused, but the wolf said, "If you don't do it, I will eat you up!" Then the miller was afraid, and he made the wolf's paws white.

The wolf knocked at the goats' door a third time and said, "Open the door, dear children, your mother is here, and I have brought something back from the forest for each of you."

The little goats cried, "First show us your feet so we will know that you are not the wolf!"

The wolf put his paws against the window. The goats saw they were white, and they believed all he said and opened the door. In ran the wolf! The little goats were terrified. One sprang under the table, the second into the bed, the third into the cold stove, the fourth behind the kitchen door, the fifth into the cupboard, the sixth under the sink, and the seventh inside the grandfather clock. But the wolf came and found them. He swallowed them one after the other. The youngest goat, hidden inside the grandfather clock, was the only one he did not find.

When the wolf was full, he went and lay down under a tree in the green meadow outside, and slept.

Soon afterwards, the mother goat came home. The door of her house stood wide open. The table, chairs and benches were thrown about, the sink was cracked, and quilts and pillows were pulled off the bed. Her children were nowhere to be found. She called them by name, one after another, but no one answered. At last, when she called the name of the youngest, a soft voice replied, "Mother, I am in the clock." She took the little goat out, and he told her that the wolf had tricked them, and had eaten all the others. You can imagine how the mother goat wept for her poor children.

After a while, they went outside, where they found the wolf under a tree, snoring. The mother goat looked closely and saw that something was moving and struggling in his fat belly. "Is it possible," she said, "that my poor swallowed children are still alive?" The youngest goat ran to fetch scissors, a needle and thread. The mother goat cut open the wolf's stomach while he slept so heavily. All six little goats sprang out, one after another. They were all still alive, because in his greediness the wolf had swallowed them whole. They were so happy!

Then the mother goat said, "Go and look for some big stones, and we will use them to fill the wolf's stomach." The seven little goats hauled the stones with all their strength, and crammed them into the wolf's stomach. Their mother quickly sewed him up again. He did not stir.

Some time later, the wolf woke up and he felt very thirsty because his stomach was full of dry stones. He decided to go to the well for a drink, but when he began to move, the stones in his stomach rattled. He cried out,

What rumbles and tumbles
Against my poor bones?
I ate six small goats,
But they now feel like stones!

When he got to the well and leaned over the water to drink, the heavy stones made him fall in! The wolf sank and drowned.

The seven little goats saw and came running. They shouted, "The wolf is dead! The wolf is dead!" and danced for joy around the well with their mother.

3

Brother and Sister

Alittle brother took his little sister by the hand and said, "Since our mother died we have been miserable. Our stepmother beats us every day, and feeds us nothing but hard leftover crusts of bread. Heaven pity us. Come, let's run away together into the wide world."

They walked the whole day and in the evening they came to a large forest. Tired out with sorrow, hunger and walking, they slept.

When they woke the next day, the sun was already hot and high in the sky. The brother said, "Sister, I am thirsty; I need to drink and I think I hear a little running brook." They set off to find water.

But their wicked stepmother was a witch. She had crept after the escaping children and bewitched all the brooks in the forest.

The brother and sister found a little brook leaping brightly over stones. The brother was going to drink from it, but the sister heard the brook say, "Who drinks from me will be a tiger; who drinks from me will be a tiger."

She cried, "Dear Brother, do not drink this water, or you will become a wild beast, and tear me to pieces."

The thirsty brother did not drink. He said, "I will wait for the next little brook."

When they came to the next brook the sister heard it say, "Who drinks from me will be a wolf; who drinks from me will be a wolf."

She cried out, "Dear Brother, do not drink this water, or you will become a wolf, and eat me."

The brother did not drink. He said, "I will wait until we come to the next brook, but then I must drink, because I am so thirsty."

When they came to the third brook, the sister heard it say, "Who drinks from me will be a deer; who drinks from me will be a deer."

She said, "Oh, dear Brother, do not drink this water, or you will become a deer, and run away from me."

But the brother had already knelt down by the brook. He drank, and as soon as the first drops touched his lips, he became a young roebuck deer.

The sister wept over her poor bewitched brother, and the deer wept too. At last the girl said, "Little roebuck deer, I will never, never leave you." She untied her golden belt and put it round the deer's neck, and she wove rushes into a soft cord to make a lead. Holding this, she walked on, deeper into the forest.

After they had travelled a long way, they came to a little cottage. The sister looked in and saw it was empty, and she decided they would stay there. She found leaves and moss to make a soft bed for the deer. Every morning she gathered roots, berries and nuts for herself, and brought tender grass for the deer, who ate out of her hand and played around her. At night, the sister laid her head upon the deer's back for a pillow, and slept softly. If only the brother had been his normal self it would have been a delightful life.

For some time they were alone like this in the wilderness. But then the King of the country held a great hunt in the forest. The bugle horn blasts, the dogs' barking and the huntsmen's merry shouts rang through the trees. The deer heard them, and was overcome by a great longing. "Oh," he said to his sister, "let me go to the hunt, I cannot bear it any longer," and he begged so much that at last she agreed.

"But," she said to him, "come back in the evening. Knock at the door and say, 'My little Sister, let me in!' That way I will know you. If you do not say that, I will not open the door." Then the young deer sprang off, happy in the open air.

The King and the huntsmen saw the pretty creature with the golden collar, and chased after him, but they could not catch him, and when they thought that they surely had him, away he sprang through the bushes. Once it was dark he ran to the cottage.

He did not know, but one huntsman had quietly followed him. The huntsman hid and watched while the deer knocked at the door and called out, "My little Sister, let me in." The huntsman saw the door open. The deer jumped inside and rested the whole night on his soft bed.

The King's huntsman went to the King and told him what he had seen and heard.

The King said, "Tomorrow we will hunt once more."

When the deer heard the bugle horn again and the "Ho! Ho!" of the huntsmen, he had no peace.

The sister begged him to stay, saying, "This time they

will kill you, and I will be alone in the forest. I will not let you out."

"Then you will have me die of grief," answered the deer. "When I hear the bugle horns I feel as if I will jump out of my skin."

So the sister opened the door for him with a heavy heart, saying, "Return in the evening and say your password." The deer, full of joy, bounded into the forest.

When the King saw the pretty deer with the golden collar, he said to his men, "Chase him all day long till nightfall, but take care that no one does him any harm."

Then as soon as the sun had set, the King asked his huntsman to show him the cottage. He knocked and called out, "My little Sister, let me in." The door opened, the King walked in, and there stood the most lovely girl he had ever seen.

At first, the sister was frightened seeing a man with a golden crown upon his head, instead of her little deer. But the King looked at her kindly, stretched out his hand, and said, "Will you come with me to my palace and be my beloved wife?"

"Yes, I will," answered the sister, "but the little deer must come with me; I cannot leave him."

The King said, "He shall stay with you as long as you live, and shall have everything he needs."

Just then, the deer came running in. The sister tied him with the cord of rushes, took it in her hand, and they went away with the King, who married the lovely girl with pomp and ceremony. She was now the Queen, and they lived for a long time happily together. The deer was cherished, and ran about in the palace garden.

Now, the stepmother witch, who the children had escaped from, thought all this time that the sister must have been torn to pieces by wild beasts in the forest, and that the brother would have been shot by the huntsmen. When she heard that they were living happily in the King's palace, envy and hatred rose in her heart. She thought of nothing but how she could bring them misfortune. Her own daughter, who was as ugly as night and had only one eye, grumbled, saying, "She, Queen! I ought to have been Queen!"

"Be quiet," answered the witch, "when a chance comes, I shall be ready."

Time went on, and it happened that one day when the King was away from the palace hunting, the Queen gave birth to a pretty baby boy.

The witch pretended to be a chambermaid. She went into the room where the Queen lay and said to her, "Come, I have prepared a hot, hot bath. It will rebuild your strength. Hurry, before it gets cold."

The witch and her one-eyed daughter carried the weak Queen into the bathroom. They put her into a hot, hot bath, then shut the door and ran away. They had made a fire in the room of such deadly heat that the beautiful young Queen soon died.

When this was done, the old witch took her daughter, put a nightcap on her head, and told her to lie in the Queen's bed. She gave her the shape and the look of the Queen, only she could not change her lost eye. She told her daughter to lie on that side so that the King would not see the missing eye.

In the evening when the King came home and heard he had a son, he was very happy. He did not realise that a false Queen was lying in the bed.

That night, at midnight, when everyone else slept, the nurse sitting by the baby's cradle saw the door open and the true Queen appeared, like a ghost. The nurse slipped out to tell the King, who crept into the room to hide and watch.

The ghostly Queen took the baby boy out of the cradle, laid him on her arm, and fed him. Then she shook up the baby's pillow, laid him down again, and covered him with the little quilt. Nor did she forget the deer. She went into the corner where he lay, and stroked his back.

As she turned to go, the King could not restrain himself: he said, "You can be none other than my dear wife."

She answered, "Yes, I am your dear wife," and at that same moment she came to life again, and by God's grace became fresh, rosy and full of health. She told the King about the witch and her daughter's evil deed.

The King ordered that they both be tried, and judgment was delivered against them. The witch's daughter was taken into the forest where she was torn to pieces by wild beasts. The witch was cast into a fire and burnt. As soon as she was burnt, the deer changed shape, returning to his human form. So the King, the sister, the brother and the baby boy lived happily in the palace together forever after.

4

Rapunzel

Once there was a man and a woman who longed for a child. They waited many years, and eventually the woman found out she was having a baby.

At the back of their house was a little window from which they could see a splendid garden full of the most beautiful flowers and herbs. The garden was surrounded by a high wall, and no one dared go into it because it belonged to an enchantress, who had great power and everyone lived in fear of her.

One day, the pregnant woman was standing by this window looking down into the garden, and she saw a flowerbed planted with a beautiful plant, a kind of rampion called "rapunzel". It looked so fresh and green that she desperately wanted to eat some. This desire increased every day. She grew weak, and began to look pale and miserable. She said to her husband. "If I can't eat some of the rapunzel growing in the garden behind our house, I shall die."

The man loved her, and decided he must bring her some of the plant, no matter what the consequences. At twilight, he clambered over the high wall into the garden of the enchantress, hastily picked a handful of rapunzel, and took it to his wife. Straightaway she made a salad from it, and ate it greedily. It tasted so delicious that the next day she longed for it three times as much as before. In the gloom of evening, her husband let himself down again into the garden.

But, turning from the wall, he was terribly afraid, for the angry enchantress was standing before him. She said, "How dare you climb into my garden and steal my rapunzel? You shall suffer for this!"

"Please," he answered, "be merciful. My wife saw your rapunzel from the window, and felt such a longing for it that she would have died if she had not been able to eat some."

Then the enchantress allowed her anger to soften, and said to him: "I will let you take the rapunzel, but I make one condition: you must give me your child when it is born. It shall be well treated; I will care for it like a mother."

In his terror, the man consented to everything.

When the baby was born, the enchantress appeared at once. She gave the child the name of Rapunzel, and took her away.

Rapunzel grew into the most beautiful girl under the sun. When she was twelve years old, the enchantress shut her

up in a tower deep in a forest. It had no door and no stairs. Right at the top was a little window. When the enchantress wanted to get in, she stood below the window and cried, "Rapunzel, Rapunzel, let down your hair."

Rapunzel had magnificent long, long hair, fine as spun gold. When she heard the voice of the enchantress, she unwound her braids and looped her hair over a hook above the window. It hung all the way to the ground, and the enchantress climbed up it.

Rapunzel had lived in the tower for four years when the King's son happened to ride close by through the forest one day. He heard a song that was so charming he stopped to listen. It was Rapunzel, passing the time in her solitude by singing with her sweet voice. The King's son looked for a door to the tower, but could not find one. The singing touched his heart and he stayed to listen.

From behind a tree, he saw the enchantress arrive and cry: "Rapunzel, Rapunzel, let down your hair." Rapunzel let down the braids of her hair, and the enchantress climbed up.

"If that is the ladder, I too will try," said the King's son.

The next day when it began to grow dark, he went to the tower and cried, "Rapunzel, Rapunzel, let down your hair." Immediately the hair fell down and the King's son climbed up.

At first Rapunzel was terribly frightened by a man she had never seen before stepping through her window, but the King's son spoke to her like a friend, and told her that his heart had been stirred by her singing. Rapunzel lost her fear. She saw that he was young and handsome. When he asked if she would marry him, she said yes, and laid her hand in his.

"I want to go away with you, but I can't get down. Bring some silk thread every time you come, and I will weave a ladder with it. Then we will ride away together on your horse." They agreed that until that time he should come every evening, for the old enchantress always came in the day.

The enchantress knew nothing of this, until one day Rapunzel asked her, "Why is it that you are so much heavier for me to pull up the tower than the King's son?"

"Ah! You wicked child!" cried the enchantress. "What do I hear you say? I thought I had separated you from all the world, and yet you have deceived me!"

In her anger she clutched Rapunzel's beautiful braids, wrapped them twice round her left hand, seized a pair of scissors with the right, and snip, snip, she cut them off! Then she took poor Rapunzel into a desert and left her there, sad and miserable.

The enchantress fastened the cut-off braids of hair to the hook over the window. When the King's son came and cried, "Rapunzel, Rapunzel, let down your hair," she dropped them down the tower. The King's son climbed up, but instead of meeting with his dearest Rapunzel, he found the wicked and venomous enchantress.

"Aha!" she cried mockingly, "You've come to fetch your dearest, but the beautiful bird no longer sits singing in the nest. The cat has got it, and will scratch out your eyes as well. You will never see Rapunzel again."

The King's son was beside himself with sorrow. In his despair he leapt down from the tower. He escaped with his life, but he fell into thorns, which pierced his eyes. He wandered quite blind through the forest, eating nothing but roots and berries, weeping over the loss of his dearest Rapunzel.

He roamed in misery like this for years, until finally he came to the desert where sad Rapunzel lived. He heard a voice, and it seemed so familiar to him that he went towards it, and Rapunzel recognised him and fell on his neck and wept. Two of her tears wetted his eyes and they grew clear again, and he could see once more. He led her to his kingdom, where he was joyfully received, and they lived for a long time afterwards, happy and contented.

5

The Three Little Men in the Wood

Once there was a man whose wife died, and a woman whose husband died. They each had a daughter.

The woman said to the man's daughter, "Tell your father that I would like to marry him. If he and I marry, you will have milk every morning to wash in, and you will drink wine, while my own daughter will wash herself in water and drink water." The girl went home, and told her father what the woman had said.

The man said, "I don't know what to do. Marriage is a joy and also a torment." He could not decide, so at length he pulled off his boot, and said, "Take this boot with a hole in it, hang it on a big nail, and pour water into it. If it holds the water, then I will marry the woman, but if the water runs through, I won't." The girl did this, and the hole in the boot blocked up and the boot filled. The girl told her father, who went to the woman and married her.

The morning after the marriage, when the two girls woke up, there in front of the man's daughter was milk for her to wash in and wine for her to drink, as the woman had promised. In front of the woman's daughter was water to wash in and water for drinking. But on the second morning, both daughters had only water. And on the third morning, the woman's daughter had milk and wine, but the man's daughter had only water. The woman became bitterly unkind to her stepdaughter. She was envious because her stepdaughter was beautiful and lovable, and her own daughter was ugly and repulsive.

In winter, when everything was frozen as hard as a stone and covered with snow, the woman made a dress out of paper. She called her stepdaughter and said, "Here, put on this dress, go out into the wood and fetch me a little basketful of strawberries."

"Good heavens!" said the girl, "Strawberries don't grow in winter! The ground is frozen, and snow has covered everything. And why am I to go in this paper dress? It is so cold outside that breath freezes! The wind will blow right through the paper."

"Are you daring to contradict me?" asked the stepmother. "Do not show your face again until you have a basket of strawberries!" Then she gave the man's daughter a little piece of hard bread, and said, "This will last you for the day." What she thought inside was, *You will die of cold and hunger, and I will never see you again.*

The man's daughter was obedient. She put on the paper dress, and went out with the basket. Far and wide there was nothing but snow. When she got into the wood she saw a small house, with three little dwarfs peeping out the windows. She knocked modestly at the door, and wished them good day. They cried, "Come in." She entered the room and seated herself on a bench by the

stove, where she began to warm herself and eat her piece of hard bread.

The dwarfs said, "Can we have some too?"

"Of course," she said, and gave them half.

They asked, "What are you doing here in the winter forest in such a thin dress?"

"Ah," she answered, "I am looking for a basket of strawberries, and cannot go home until I have found them."

When she had eaten her bread, the dwarfs gave her a broom and said, "Sweep away the snow at the back door for us."

Once she'd gone outside, they said to each other, "What shall we give her? She is so good, and has shared her bread with us."

The first said, "My gift is that she shall grow more beautiful every day."

The second said, "My gift is that every time she speaks, gold pieces will fall out of her mouth."

The third said, "My gift is a King who will love and marry her."

The girl swept away the snow behind the little house, and what did she find but ripe strawberries, dark red in the white world! Joyfully she gathered her basketful, thanked the little men, and ran home to deliver the berries to her stepmother.

When she went in and said hello, a piece of gold fell out of her mouth. She told what had happened to her in the wood, and with every word she spoke, gold pieces fell from her mouth, until very soon the whole room was covered with them.

"Now look at her arrogance," cried the stepsister, "throwing gold around!" but really she was envious, and wanted to seek strawberries in the forest also.

Her mother said, "No, my dear daughter, you might die of cold." But her daughter still wanted to go, and at last the mother gave in. She made her own daughter a magnificent dress of fur, and gave her bread and butter and cake to take.

The girl went straight to the little house in the forest. The three dwarfs peeped out, but she did not greet them. Without speaking to them, she barged into their room, seated herself by the stove, and began to eat her bread and butter and cake.

"Give us some bread and cake," cried the little men.

But the woman's daughter replied, "There's only enough for me, so I cannot give any away."

When she had finished eating, the dwarfs said, "Here is a broom; please sweep the snow away from the back door for us."

"Humph! Sweep for yourselves," she answered, "I am not your servant." When she saw that they were not going to make gold fall from her mouth, she left.

The little men said to each other, "What shall we give her? She is so rude and has a wicked, envious heart, and won't do a good turn for anyone else."

The first said, "My gift is that she will grow uglier every day."

The second said, "My gift is that every time she speaks, a toad will spring out of her mouth."

The third said, "My gift is that she will die a miserable death."

The mother's daughter looked for strawberries in the forest, but didn't find any. She went angrily home. She began to tell her mother what had happened, but whenever she spoke, a toad sprang out of her mouth, to everyone's horror.

Her mother became still more enraged. She thought only of how to harm her husband's daughter, whose beauty grew more remarkable every day.

One day the woman told her stepdaughter to rinse yarn by chopping a hole in the ice of the frozen river. The girl went out and cut the hole, but then a splendid carriage drove up. It belonged to the King.

The carriage stopped, and the King asked, "Beautiful one, who are you, and what are you doing?"

"I am a poor girl, and I am rinsing yarn."

The King felt compassion for the girl, and he fell in love with her face. He said to her, "Would you come away and marry me?"

"Yes, with all my heart," she answered, for she was glad to get away from her stepmother and stepsister. She travelled with the King to his palace where they had a magnificent wedding.

A year later, the young Queen had a son. Her stepmother had heard of her good fortune. She came with her daughter to the palace and pretended that she wanted to pay the young Queen a visit. But when the King had gone out and there was no one else around, the wicked woman seized the Queen's head, and her daughter seized the Queen's feet. They lifted her out of bed and threw her out of the window into a stream below. Then the ugly daughter lay in the bed, and the woman covered her up, right over her head.

When the King returned home, the woman told him his Queen was unwell and that he must let her rest. The King suspected no evil, and did not come back till next morning. Then he talked with his wife but when she answered him, toads leapt from the bed, instead of gold pieces. He asked what this could mean, but the woman said it was just the illness and it would soon stop.

During the night, the palace kitchen boy saw a duck come swimming up the stream. It came in and asked, "Where is my baby?"

He answered, "The baby is sleeping in his cradle."

Then the duck took the form of the Queen and went upstairs to nurse the baby. Once she'd tucked the baby back into bed, she swam away again in the shape of a duck. She came again the next night. Then on the third night she said to the kitchen boy, "Go and tell the King to swing his sword three times above me." The kitchen boy ran and got the King, who came with his sword and did as the duck had asked. At the third swing, his wife stood before him, strong and healthy, as she had been before. The King was amazed and joyful.

The next day he called the Queen's stepmother before him and asked her, "What does a person deserve who drags someone out of bed and throws them in the water?"

"A wretch like that would deserve nothing better," answered the woman, "than to be put in a barrel stuck full of nails, and rolled downhill into the river."

The King said, "You have pronounced your own sentence." He ordered such a barrel to be brought, and the woman to be put into it with her daughter, and then the top was hammered on, and the barrel rolled downhill to the river.

6

Hansel and Gretel

A poor woodcutter lived with his two children, Hansel and Gretel, beside a large forest. The children's mother had died but, after a time, the woodcutter married again.

There was never much to eat in the house, but then came a famine and there wasn't even enough bread for the four of them.

One night, the woodcutter lay in bed, tossing and turning with worry. He sighed and said to his wife, "What will happen to us? How can we feed my poor children when we have barely enough for ourselves?"

His wife answered, "Listen. Tomorrow we'll take the children deep into the forest and give them each a piece of bread. Then we'll leave them there. They'll never find the way home, and that way we won't need to feed them."

"No, wife," said the man. "I won't do it. How could I leave my children alone in the woods? Wild animals would come and tear them to pieces."

"You fool!" she said. "Then all four of us will starve." And she gave him no peace until he agreed.

The children were too hungry to sleep, so they had overheard their stepmother. Gretel began crying and said, "Oh, Hansel. There's no hope for us."

"Don't worry, Gretel," said Hansel, "I'll find a way."

When the grown-ups were asleep, he got up, put on his jacket and crept outside. The moon was shining bright, and the pebbles on the ground glittered like silver coins. Hansel stuffed his pockets full of them.

At daybreak, the stepmother came and woke the children. "Get up, you lazy, selfish children. We're going to the forest for wood." Then she handed them each a piece of bread and said, "This is for your lunch. Don't eat it too soon; there won't be any more." Gretel put the bread in her apron, because Hansel had his pockets full of pebbles.

Then they all set out for the forest. But Hansel kept stopping and looking back. Each time he turned, he took a shiny pebble from his pocket and dropped it on the ground.

When they came to the middle of the forest, their father said, "Start gathering wood, children, and I'll make a fire to keep you warm."

Hansel and Gretel gathered twigs till they had a good pile. The fire was lit and, when the flames were high enough, the stepmother said, "Now, children, lie down here and rest. We're going into the forest to cut wood. When we're done, we'll come back and get you."

Hansel and Gretel sat by the fire, and at midday they ate their pieces of bread. They heard strokes of an axe and thought their father was nearby. But it wasn't an axe, it was a branch he had tied to a dead tree, so it would sound like chopping when the wind blew it to and fro.

After some time, they were so tired that their eyes closed and they fell asleep. When at last they awoke, night had fallen. Gretel began to cry and said, "How will we ever get out of this forest?"

But Hansel comforted her. "Just wait a little while. As soon as the moon rises, we'll find the way." And when the full moon had risen, Hansel took his little sister by the hand and followed the pebbles, which glistened like silver pieces and showed them the way home.

They walked all night and reached their father's house as day was breaking. When the stepmother opened the door and saw them, she cried, "Wicked children! Why did you stay so long in the forest?" But their father was overjoyed, for he had been very unhappy since leaving them.

Time passed and the famine continued. The children heard their stepmother talking to their father in bed. "Everything has been eaten; we have only half a loaf of bread left. The children must go. We'll take them even deeper into the forest, and this time they won't find their way home. It's our only hope."

The husband was heavy hearted. He thought it would be better to share his last bite with his children. But the stepmother wouldn't listen and only scolded him. Once you've said yes, it's hard to say no, and so the woodcutter gave in again.

The children were awake and heard the conversation. When the grown-ups were asleep, Hansel got up again. He wanted to gather more pebbles, but the stepmother had locked the door so he couldn't get out. Still, he comforted his little sister, saying, "Don't cry, Gretel. God will help us."

Early in the morning, the stepmother came and got the children out of bed. She gave them their pieces of bread, but this time smaller than before. On the way through the forest,

Hansel kept turning back and dropping a few breadcrumbs on the ground.

The stepmother led the children to a place deep in the forest, where they had never been before. Again they made a fire, and she said, "Just sit here, children. If you get tired you can sleep. We're going to cut wood, and this evening when we've finished, we'll come and get you."

At midday, Gretel shared her bread with Hansel, as he had scattered his on the ground. They fell asleep and the afternoon passed, but no one came for the poor children.

It was after dark when they woke, and Hansel comforted his little sister. "Gretel," he said, "just wait till the moon rises. Then we'll see the breadcrumbs I scattered and they'll show us the way home."

When the moon rose, they set out, but they didn't find any breadcrumbs because all the birds of the forest had eaten them up. Hansel said to Gretel, "Don't worry, we'll find the way." But they didn't find it.

They walked all night, and then all day from morning to night, and they were very hungry, for they had eaten only a few berries they picked from the bushes. When they were so tired their legs could carry them no further, they lay down under a tree and fell asleep.

Now it was the third morning since they had left their father's house. They started out again, but wandered even deeper and deeper into the forest and, unless help came soon, they were sure to die of hunger and weariness.

At midday, they saw a lovely snowbird sitting on a branch, singing so beautifully that they stood still and listened. Then it flapped its wings and flew on ahead, and they followed until the bird came to a little house and perched on the roof.

Coming closer, they saw that the house was made of gingerbread, and the roof was made of cake and the windows of sparkling sugar. "Let's eat some," said Hansel. "I'll take a piece of the roof. You, Gretel, try some of the window. It looks sweet."

Hansel reached up and broke off a bit of the roof to see how it tasted, and Gretel pressed against the windowpanes and nibbled at them. Then a soft voice called from inside, "Nibble nibble, little mouse, who's that nibbling at my house?"

The children answered, "It is only the wind, so wild." And they carried on eating. Hansel so liked the taste of the roof, he broke off a big chunk, and Gretel took out a whole windowpane and sat down on the ground to enjoy it.

All at once, the door opened, and an old woman came hobbling out. Hansel and Gretel were so frightened, they dropped what they were eating. But the old woman nodded her head and said, "Oh, what dear children! However did you get here? Don't be afraid, come in and stay with me."

She took them by the hand and led them into her house. A fine meal of milk and pancakes, sugar, apples and nuts was set before them. Then two little beds were made up, clean and white, and Hansel and Gretel got into them and thought they were in heaven.

But the old woman had only pretended to be kind. She was really a wicked witch who tempted children in to her house and then killed, cooked, and ate them up. She had built her house out of gingerbread to entice them. Witches have red eyes and can't see very far, but they have a keen sense of smell and know when humans are coming.

Early the next morning, the witch got up, and when she saw the children sleeping, she muttered to herself, "What tasty morsels they will be!" She grabbed Hansel with her scrawny hand, carried him to a little shed and bolted the door. He screamed as loud as he could, but no one heard him.

Then the witch went back to Gretel, shook her awake and cried, "Get up, lazy, selfish child. You must fetch water and cook something for your brother. He's locked in the shed and we will fatten him up. When he's nice and plump, I shall eat him." Gretel wept bitterly, but she had to do what the wicked witch told her.

Every morning the witch went to the shed and said, "Hansel, hold out your finger. Let's feel how fat you are getting." But Hansel held out a bone. Because she couldn't see well, she thought it was his finger. She wondered why he stayed so thin.

When four weeks had gone by and the boy was skinny as ever, she decided not to wait any longer. "Gretel," she cried out. "Fetch water and don't dawdle. Skinny or fat, I'm going to cook Hansel up tomorrow."

The little girl wailed, and tears flowed down her cheeks! "Dear God," she cried, "won't you help us?"

"Stop that blubbering," said the witch. "It won't do you a bit of good."

Early in the morning, Gretel had to fill the kettle with water and light the fire. "First we'll do some baking," said the old witch. "I've heated the oven and kneaded the dough." And she took poor Gretel out to the oven, which by now was spitting flames.

"Crawl in," said the witch, "and see if it's hot enough for bread."

The witch was going to close the door on Gretel and roast her, so she could eat her too. But Gretel guessed what she must be thinking and said, "I don't know how to get in."

"Silly goose," said the witch. "The door is big enough. Look. Even I can get in." She crept to the oven and stuck her head in. At that moment Gretel gave her a great push, closed the iron door and fastened the bolt. How horribly the witch screeched as she burnt to death.

Gretel ran straight to Hansel, opened the door of the shed, and cried, "Hansel, we're saved! The witch is dead."

Hansel hopped out like a bird freed from its cage. How happy they were! They hugged and kissed each other and danced around. Now there was nothing to be afraid of, they went into the witch's house and in every corner they found boxes of pearls and precious stones. Hansel stuffed his pockets full of them saying, "These will be much better than pebbles." Gretel, too, filled her apron with them.

"We'd better leave now," said Hansel, "and get out of this bewitched forest."

They walked a long way, and came to a body of water. "How will we get across?" said Hansel. "There's no bridge."

"And no boat either," said Gretel. "But over there I see a white duck. She'll help us." She cried out, "Duckling, please give us a ride."

Sure enough, the duck came to them and took them across, one at a time.

When they were safely over and had walked on some way, the forest looked more and more familiar, and finally they saw their home in the distance. They began to run. They flew into the house and threw themselves into their father's arms.

The poor man hadn't had a happy hour since he had left the children in the forest, and in the meantime his wife had died. Gretel opened out her little apron, and the pearls and precious stones went bouncing around the room. Hansel reached into his pockets and tossed out handful after handful. Now all their worries were over, and they lived together happily ever after.

7

The Fisherman and his Wife

Once upon a time there was a fisherman who lived with his wife in a miserable shack close by the sea. One day as he was sitting with his fishing rod, looking at the clear water, his line suddenly went down, and when he pulled it up again, he had caught a large flounder fish.

The flounder said to him, "Fisherman, please, let me live! I am not a flounder really, but an enchanted prince. I would not be good to eat; put me in the water again, and let me go."

The fisherman said, "There is no need to say so much about it – of course I would let go any fish that could talk." He put the flounder back into the clear water, and then he went home to his wife, who was called Ilsalont.

"Husband," said Ilsalont, "didn't you catch anything today?"

"No," said the man. "Well, I did catch a flounder, but he said he was an enchanted prince, so I let him go again."

"Didn't you wish for anything first?"

"No, what would I wish for?"

"Ah," said the woman, "it is hard to live every day in this dirty shack; you could have wished for a cottage. Go back and call him. Tell him we want to have a small cottage, he will certainly give us that."

"Oh," said the man, "I'm not sure it's right to call him back and ask for something."

"Now look," said the woman, "because you caught him, and you let him go again, he is sure to do it. Go at once."

The man still did not like this plan, but he also didn't like to oppose his wife, so he went to the sea.

When he got there, the water was green and yellow, and its smooth surface was now ruffled. He stood at the edge and said,

> Flounder, flounder in the sea,
> Come, I ask you, here to me;
> For my good wife, Ilsalont,
> Wants not as I'd wish she'd want.

The flounder came swimming to him. "Well, what is it that she wants?"

The man said, "I did catch you, and my wife says I really ought to have wished for something. She does not like living in a wretched shack; she would like to have a cottage."

"Go, then," said the flounder, "she has it already."

When the man went home, his wife was no longer in the shack but instead, where it had been, there was a lovely little cottage, and she was sitting on a bench beside the door. She took him by the hand saying, "Look, this is much better, isn't it?"

They went in, and there was a small porch, and a pretty little parlour and bedroom, and a kitchen and pantry, with

the best of furniture, and beautiful things made of tin and brass – everything you could want. Behind the cottage there was a small yard with hens and ducks, and a little garden with flowers and fruit. "Look," said the wife, "isn't it nice?"

"Yes," said the husband, "and so, from now on, we will be quite contented."

"Let's wait and see," said the wife.

Everything went well for a week or so, and then the woman said, "Listen, husband, this cottage is far too small for us, and the garden and yard are also small; the flounder could just as easily have given us a larger house. I would like to live in a great stone castle; go to the flounder, and tell him to give us a castle."

"Ah, wife," said the man, "this cottage is good enough; why should we live in a castle?"

"Just go and ask. The flounder can do it," said the woman.

The man's heart grew heavy. He said to himself, "It is not right to ask for more. The flounder has only just given us this cottage." And yet he went.

When he came to the sea, the water was now purple, dark blue and grey, and thick. He stood there and said,

> Flounder, flounder in the sea,
> Come, I ask you, here to me;
> For my good wife, Ilsalont,
> Wants not as I'd wish she'd want.

"Well, what does she want, then?" said the flounder.

"Alas," said the man, half scared, "she wants to live in a great stone castle."

"Go to it," said the flounder, "she is standing before the door."

Then the man went home, but when he got there he found a great stone castle, and his wife was waiting on the steps. She took him by the hand and said, "Come in."

In the castle was a vast hall paved with marble, and many servants, who flung wide the doors, and the walls were all bright with beautiful hangings, and in the rooms were chairs and tables of pure gold, and crystal chandeliers hung from the ceiling, and all the rooms and bedrooms had carpets, and the very best food and wine was laid out on all the tables so that they nearly sagged with the weight. Behind the castle, there was a great courtyard, with stables for horses and cows, and the very best carriages. There was a magnificent, large garden too, with the most beautiful flowers and fruit trees, and a park half-a-mile long, in which there were stags, deer and everything that could be desired.

"Isn't it beautiful?" said the woman.

"Yes, indeed," said the man, "now let it be; we will live in this castle and be content."

"Let's wait and see," asked the woman.

Next morning, the wife woke first. From her bed she saw the beautiful landscape through their window. She poked her husband in the side with her elbow, and said, "Get up, husband, and look out the window. Couldn't we be the King over all that land? Go to the flounder, it will make us King."

"Ah, wife," said the man, "why should we be King? I do not want to be King."

"Well," said the wife, "if you won't be King, I will. Go to the flounder!"

"Why do you want to be King?" asked the man, "I do not want to ask him for more."

"Why not?" said the woman. "Go to him this instant; I must be King!"

It is not right; it is not right, thought the man. He did not want to go, yet he went.

When he came to the sea, it was dark grey. The water heaved up from below, and smelt foul. He went and stood by it, and said,

> Flounder, flounder in the sea,
> Come, I ask you, here to me;
> For my good wife, Ilsalont,
> Wants not as I'd wish she'd want.

"Well, what does she want, then?" said the flounder.

"Alas," said the man, "she wants to be King."

"Go to her; she is King already."

So the man went, and where the castle had been he found a palace. It had a great tower and magnificent ornaments, and there were soldiers with kettle drums and trumpets. When he went inside the palace, everything was real marble and gold, with velvet covers and golden tassels. Then the doors of the hall were opened, and there was the court in all its splendour, and his wife was sitting on a high throne of gold and diamonds, with a great crown of gold on her head, and a sceptre of pure gold and jewels in her hand, and on both sides of her stood her maids-in-waiting in a row, each of them always one head shorter than the last.

The man went and stood before her, and said, "Ah, wife, now you are King."

"Yes," said the woman, "now I am King."

"Now that you are King, let all else be, now we will wish for nothing more."

"Nay, husband," said the woman, quite anxiously, "Now I am King, I find time passes very heavily, I can bear it no longer. Go to the flounder – I must be Pope, too."

"Alas, wife," said the man, "it cannot make you Pope, and I cannot ask it. It is too much. There is one Pope in all of Christendom."

"What!" said the woman, "I am the King. You are nothing but my husband. I command you to go at once! If he can make me King, he can make me Pope. I must be Pope this very day!"

So the man was forced to go. As he went, he was troubled in mind and his knees trembled. He thought to himself, *It will not end well; it will not end well! Pope is too shameless! The flounder will become tired out.*

A high wind blew over the land, and the clouds flew, and towards evening all grew dark. Leaves fell from the trees, and the water rose and roared as if it were boiling, and splashed upon the shore. Full of despair and fear, the fisherman went and said,

> Flounder, flounder in the sea,
> Come, I ask you, here to me;
> For my good wife, Ilsalont,
> Wants not as I'd wish she'd want.

"Well, what does she want, then?" asked the flounder.

"Alas," said the man, "she wants to be Pope."

"Go to her then," said the flounder; "she is Pope already."

So he went, and he saw a cathedral surrounded by palaces. He pushed his way through the crowd. Inside, everything was lit up with thousands and thousands of candles. His wife was clad in gold, and she was sitting on a much higher throne, and had three great golden crowns on. All the emperors and kings were on their knees before her, kissing her shoes. "Wife," said the man, looking attentively at her, "are you now Pope?"

"Yes," said she, "I am Pope." So he stood and looked at her, and it was just as if he was looking at the bright sun. When he had stood looking at her for a short time, he said, "Ah, wife, if you are Pope, be satisfied. You cannot become anything greater now; let that be enough."

"Let's wait and see," said the woman.

Thereupon they both went to bed. But the wife was not satisfied, and greediness let her have no sleep, for she was continually thinking about what there was left for her to be. At length the sun began to rise, and when the woman saw the light of dawn, she sat up in bed. She said, "Cannot I, too, order the sun and moon to rise? Husband," she said, poking him in the ribs with her elbow, "wake up! Go to the flounder, for I wish to be as powerful as God."

The man was still half asleep, but he was so horrified that he fell out of bed. He said, "Alas, wife, what are you saying?"

"Husband," she said, "if I can't order the sun and moon to rise, I can't bear it. I shall not know what it is to have another happy hour, unless I can make them rise myself." Then she looked at him so terribly that a shudder ran over him, and she said, "Go at once; I wish to be like God."

"But wife," said the man, falling on his knees before her, "the flounder cannot do that; I beseech you, go on as you are, and be Pope."

Then she fell into a rage, and her hair flew wildly about her head, and she cried, "I will not endure this, I'll not bear it any longer: go!"

He put on his trousers and ran away like a madman. Outside, a great storm was raging and blowing so hard that he could scarcely keep upright; houses and trees toppled over, the mountains trembled, rocks rolled into the sea, the sky was pitch black, with thunder and lightening, and the sea came in with black waves as high as church towers, and all with crests of white foam at the top. The fisherman cried out, though he could not hear his own words,

> Flounder, flounder in the sea,
> Come, I ask you, here to me;
> For my good wife, Ilsalont,
> Wants not as I'd wish she'd want.

"Well, what does she want, then?" said the flounder.

"Alas," said he, "she wants to be like God."

"Like God? Go to her, and you will find her back again in the shack."

And the fisherman and his wife still live there, even now.

8

Cinderella

A mother was very ill. She knew she would soon die, leaving behind her second husband, who was rich but not kind, and her beautiful daughter. She called her daughter to her bedside and said, "My dear girl, be good and God will protect you. I will look down on you from heaven and be near you."

After she died, the girl went to her mother's grave every day, and cried.

Winter came, and in the spring the girl's stepfather married a new wife. The new wife had two daughters, who had pretty faces but mean, jealous hearts.

These new stepsisters took the girl's lovely clothes away from her and gave her an old dress and wooden shoes to wear. "Just look at her now!" they laughed. They made her work from morning till night. She got up before the sun, carried water, lit fires, cooked and washed.

The girl didn't have a bed; she had to sleep by the fire in the cinders. This meant she always looked dusty and dirty, and so they called her "Cinderella".

Once, when their stepfather was going away to a fair, the

two stepsisters asked him to buy them pearls and jewels. Cinderella said, "Please bring me the first branch that knocks against your hat on your way home." So he brought gemstones for the two stepsisters and a hazel branch for Cinderella.

Cinderella thanked him. She planted the hazel branch beside her mother's grave and watered it with her tears. It grew, and became a beautiful tree. Cinderella would sit beneath it to cry and pray, and the birds would come to sit in the tree and listen.

One day the King of the land announced a great festival to honour his son, the prince. When the two stepsisters heard the news, they were very excited. "Come, Cinderella," they demanded, "comb our hair for us, tie our sashes and fasten our buckles, for we are going to the King's palace!"

Cinderella did everything her stepsisters asked, and then she said, "May I go to the dance too?"

"You, Cinderella!" replied her stepmother, "Go to the dance, covered in dust and dirt? You have no clothes or shoes!"

But Cinderella still wished to go.

Her stepmother tipped a great pot of lentils into the ashes, and said, "If you pick them all out before we leave, in two hours time, you can come with us."

Cinderella opened the window and called,

> Pigeons, turtle doves,
> All the birds of the sky,
> Peck lentils for the pot,
> And leave the ashes aside.

Two pigeons flew in, then the turtle doves, then all the birds from near and far came whirring and crowding into the kitchen to peck among the ashes. They gathered the good lentils back into the pot in less than an hour.

Cinderella showed the pot to her stepmother, full of delight because she thought she could go to the dance, but the cruel stepmother said, "It makes no difference. You cannot come, for you have no clothes and cannot dance. We would be ashamed of you!" She turned her back, and hurried away with her two mean, jealous daughters.

Cinderella went to her mother's grave beneath the hazel tree, and called out,

> Shiver and quiver, little tree,
> Drop silver and gold down over me.

A white bird in the tree brought down a beautiful silver ballgown, and slippers embroidered with silver silk. Cinderella quickly put them on, and went to the dance.

Everyone at the King's palace stopped to look at the beautiful stranger. Cinderella's stepsisters and stepmother didn't recognise her because she looked so much like a princess in her silver dress.

The prince was captivated. He only danced with Cinderella, and never let go of her hand.

She danced till it was late, and then she wanted to go home. The prince said, "I will accompany you," for he wished to see where the beautiful girl was from. She escaped him, however, and hid in the pigeon house. The prince waited until her stepfather came, and told him an unknown girl had leapt into the pigeon house. The stepfather brought an axe and chopped the pigeon house to pieces. No one was inside, for Cinderella had jumped quickly down from the back of the pigeon house and had run to the little hazel tree. There she had taken off her beautiful clothes and laid them on her mother's grave, and the bird had taken them away again. Then she had sat down in the kitchen among the ashes.

Next day the King's festival for his son began afresh. Cinderella went to the hazel tree and said,

> Shiver and quiver, little tree,
> Drop silver and gold down over me.

Then the bird threw down an even more gorgeous dress of gold and sparkling golden slippers. And when Cinderella appeared in this dress, everyone was astonished at her beauty. The prince had been waiting for her, and danced with no one else.

When it got late, she wished to leave, and the prince followed her, but she ran away from him, and into the garden behind the house. There stood a magnificent tall pear tree. She clambered so nimbly between the branches that the prince did not know where she had gone. He waited until her stepfather came, and told him an unknown girl had climbed the pear tree. The man took an axe and cut the tree down, but no one was in it. Cinderella had jumped down on the other side of the pear tree, had given the beautiful dress to the bird on the little hazel tree, and sat by the fire in the kitchen.

On the third day, Cinderella went once more to her mother's grave and said to the little tree:

> Shiver and quiver, little tree,
> Drop silver and gold down over me.

And now the bird threw down to her a gold and silver dress, which was more splendid and magnificent than any she had yet had, and golden slippers embroidered with silver. And when she went to the dance in the dress, no one could speak because they were so astonished. The prince danced only with her.

When Cinderella wished to leave, the prince was anxious to go with her, but she escaped from him so quickly that he could not follow. However, he had asked for the whole staircase to be smeared with sticky tar, and so, when she ran down, her left slipper stuck. The prince picked it up. It was small and dainty and glittered in the light of the moon.

The next morning, the prince declared, "I will marry the girl whose foot fits this slipper!"

He went from house to house throughout the land. He came to Cinderella's house and the eldest stepsister tried on the slipper. Her foot was far too big; she couldn't fit her toes into the shoe.

The prince passed the slipper to the second stepsister, who took it away to her room. There she got her toes safely into it, but her heel was too large. Her mother gave her a knife and said, "Cut a bit off your heel. When you are Queen, you won't be travelling on foot."

The second stepsister cut off a bit of her heel, forced her foot into the shoe, swallowed the pain, and went out to the prince. He helped her onto his horse and took her away to be his bride.

But they had to pass the tree beside Cinderella's mother's grave. There sat a pigeon, who cooed,

Turn and look, turn and look,
Blood drips from the shoe.
The slipper was too small for her,
Your true bride waits for you.

The prince turned and saw the blood trickling from the stepsister's foot. Shocked, he turned his horse around. "Who else lives here?" he demanded at the house.

"There is only the kitchen maid, Cinderella," said the stepmother. "You cannot want to see her." But the prince insisted that even the kitchen maid should try the slipper.

Cinderella washed her hands and face and went to the prince. She took her foot out of its heavy wooden shoe and slid it into the little slipper, which fitted perfectly. When she stood up, the prince looked into her eyes and recognised the beautiful girl from the dance. He shouted, "This is my true bride!"

The stepmother and the two stepsisters turned pale with astonishment and rage.

The prince helped Cinderella onto his horse and they rode away.

As they passed by the hazel tree, two pigeons cooed,

She fits the shoe,
Your bride is true,
Goodbye to you,
Goodbye to you.

Cinderella and her prince were married that day, and

they lived in his magnificent palace, where they were happy ever after.

The stepsisters attended the wedding, hoping to share in Cinderella's good fortune. But as they walked into church, pigeons pecked out their eyes, and so, for their wickedness and lies, they were punished with blindness for the rest of their days.

9

Mother Holle

There was once a widow who had a daughter who was ugly and lazy and a stepdaughter who was pretty and hard working. The widow indulged the ugly, lazy daugher, because she was her own. She made her stepdaughter do all the work around the house.

Every day the poor girl had to sit beside a well, and spin and spin till her fingers bled. One day, the shuttle she used for spinning got marked by her blood. She dipped it in the well to wash the mark off, but it dropped out of her hand and fell to the bottom. She began to weep, and ran to tell her stepmother of the mistake. But her stepmother scolded her mercilessly and declared: "Since you have let the shuttle fall in, you must fetch it out again."

The girl went back to the well and, because she felt so sad, she jumped in to get the shuttle. She fell unconscious, and when she came around again, she was in a lovely meadow where the sun was shining and many thousands of flowers were growing.

Across this meadow she went, and came to an oven full of bread. The bread cried out, "Oh, take me out or I shall burn! I have been baked a long time!" So she took out all the loaves one after another with the bread shovel.

After that she went on till she came to a tree covered with apples, which called out to her, "Oh, shake me! We apples are all ripe!" So she shook the tree till the apples fell like rain, then she gathered them into a heap and went on her way.

At last she came to a little house, out of which an old woman peeped. The old woman had such large teeth that the girl was frightened and was about to run away, but the old woman called out to her, "What are you afraid of, dear child? Stay with me. If you will do all the work in the house properly, I will reward you for it. Only you must take care to make my bed well, and to shake it thoroughly till the feathers fly, for then there is snow on the earth. I am Mother Holle."

As the old woman spoke so kindly to her, the girl felt better and agreed to work for her. She did all her chores to the satisfaction of her mistress, and always shook the bed so vigorously that the feathers flew about like snowflakes. She had a pleasant life with Mother Holle, who never spoke an angry word, and she had good meat to eat every day.

The girl stayed some time with Mother Holle, but eventually she became sad. At first she did not know why she was sad, but then she understood that it was homesickness: even though she was many thousand times better off here than with her stepmother, still she longed for her old home. At last she said to Mother Holle, "I have a longing for home, and even though I am so well off down here, I cannot stay. I must go up again to my own people."

Mother Holle said, "I am pleased that you long for your

home again, and as you have served me so well, I myself will take you up there."

She led the girl to a large door. The door opened and, just as the girl was standing in the doorway, a heavy shower of golden rain fell, and all the gold clung to her so that she was completely covered in it.

"You shall have this gold because you have been so industrious," said Mother Holle, and at the same time she gave the girl back the shuttle she had dropped into the well. Then the door closed, and the girl found herself up on the earth, not far from her stepmother's house.

She went in to her stepmother and because she arrived covered with gold, both her stepmother and stepsister were pleased to see her.

The girl told all that had happened to her. As soon as the mother heard how her stepdaughter had come by so much wealth, she was very anxious to get the same for her ugly and lazy daughter. She made her daughter sit by the well and spin. The daughter pricked her hand with a thorn to stain the shuttle, then threw it in and jumped after it.

This girl came, like the first, to the beautiful meadow. When she got to the oven, the bread again cried, "Oh, take me out or I shall burn! I have been baked a long time!" But the lazy girl answered, "I have no wish to make myself dirty!" and on she went.

Soon she came to the apple tree, which cried, "Oh, shake me! We apples are all ripe!" But she answered, "One of you might fall on my head," and she walked on.

When she came to Mother Holle's house she was not afraid, for she had already heard all about her from her stepsister, and she immediately agreed to work there.

The first day, the lazy girl forced herself to work diligently.

She obeyed Mother Holle, for she was thinking of all the gold that she would receive. But on the second day she became slower and less willing. On the third day still more so, and after that she would not get up in the morning at all. She never made Mother Holle's bed properly: she did not shake it and make the feathers fly. Mother Holle was soon tired of this, and told the girl to leave. The lazy girl thought that now the golden rain would come.

Mother Holle led her to the great door, but while she was standing beneath it, instead of the gold, a big kettleful of black tar was emptied over her.

"That is the reward for your service," said Mother Holle, and shut the door.

So the lazy girl went home, covered with black tar.

It stuck fast to her, and could not be got off as long as she lived.

10

The Seven Ravens

There was once a man who had seven sons but no daughters, though he wished very much for one. Eventually he and his wife had an eighth child, and it was a girl.

Their joy was great, but the baby was sickly and small. They were worried she might not live, so they wanted her to be baptised immediately. The father sent one of the boys to fetch water for the baptism. The other six went with him and, because each of them wanted to be first to fill it, they fought, and the jug fell into the well. None of them dared to go home.

When they didn't come back, the father said: "They have forgotten the water while playing some game, the wicked boys!" He became afraid that the girl would die without being baptised. In his anger he cried: "I wish all the boys would be turned into ravens." Hardly were the words spoken when he heard a whirring of wings over his head, and saw seven coal-black ravens flying away.

The parents were very sad and missed their seven sons. But they comforted themselves with their dear little daughter, who grew stronger and more beautiful every day.

For a long time, the girl did not know that she had had brothers, as her parents did not mention them. One day, though, she overheard some other people saying that she was beautiful, but that she was also to blame for her brothers' misfortune.

The girl was very upset. She went to her father and mother and asked if it was true that she had had brothers, and what had happened to them. The parents now knew they had to tell her, but they told her that what had happened to her brothers was the will of Heaven, and that she was not the cause.

Still, the girl thought daily of her brothers and was filled with determination to save them. She set out secretly to find them. She took nothing with her but a gold ring that had belonged to her parents, and bread and water.

She travelled far, far, to the very end of the world. She journeyed to the sun, but it was too hot and terrible. She ran to the moon, but it was too cold and malicious. She came to the stars, which were kind and good. The morning star gave her a chicken drumstick and said, "Without this drumstick, you cannot open the glass mountain, and in the glass mountain are your brothers."

The girl took the drumstick, wrapped it carefully in a cloth, and went on until she reached the glass mountain. The door was shut, so she looked for the drumstick, but when she undid the cloth, it was empty! She had lost the morning star's present. What could she do now? To rescue her brothers she needed a key to the glass mountain. The good sister took a knife, cut off one of her little fingers, put it in the door, and was able to open it.

When she had gone inside, a little dwarf came to meet her. She said to the dwarf, "I am looking for my brothers, the seven ravens."

The dwarf replied, "The lord ravens are not at home, but you can wait here for them."

Then the dwarf set out the ravens' dinner on seven little plates, and in seven little glasses. The little sister ate a morsel from each plate, and from each little glass she took a sip. In the last little glass she dropped her parents' ring. She hid behind a door and waited.

Suddenly she heard a whirring of wings and a rushing through the air, and the ravens came in. They were hungry, and went to their plates and glasses. They began to ask, "Who has eaten from my plate? Who has drunk out of my glass? It was a human mouth."

When the seventh raven finished his drink, the gold ring in his glass rolled against his beak. He took it out and recognised that it had been his mother and father's. He said, "God grant that our sister may be here, for then we shall be free."

When the girl heard that wish, she came forward to them, and all the ravens were restored to their human form. The brothers and sister embraced and kissed each other, and went joyfully home.

11

Little Red Riding Hood

Once upon a time there was a dear little girl who was loved by everyone, but most of all by her grandmother, who would have given her anything. Once, her grandmother had given her a riding hood of red velvet. She loved it and from then on would never wear anything else, so she was called Little Red Riding Hood.

One day Little Red Riding Hood's mother said to her, "Come, Little Red Riding Hood, here is a piece of cake and a bottle of wine. Take them to your grandmother, for she is ill and weak, and they will do her good. But when you are walking in the wood, do not talk to strangers and do not leave the path."

As Little Red Riding Hood walked along the path through the trees, she met a wolf. Little Red Riding Hood did not know what a wicked creature he was, so she was not at all afraid.

"Good day, Little Red Riding Hood," said the wolf.

"Good day, Wolf."

"Where are you walking, Little Red Riding Hood?"

"To my grandmother's."

"Where does your grandmother live, Little Red Riding Hood?"

"A little further on in the wood. Her house stands under the three large oak trees," replied Little Red Riding Hood.

The wolf thought, *What a tender young creature! What a nice plump mouthful! She will be better to eat than the old woman. If I act craftily, I can catch them both.* He said, "See, Little Red Riding Hood, how pretty the flowers are, here beyond the path?"

Little Red Riding Hood saw sunbeams dancing through the trees and pretty flowers growing everywhere. She decided to pick a posy to take to her grandmother, and she wandered off the path, deeper and deeper into the wood.

While she was wandering, the wolf ran straight to her grandmother's house and knocked at the door.

"Who is there?" called the grandmother.

"Little Red Riding Hood," replied the wolf. "I have cake and wine for you."

"Come in, Little Red Riding Hood," called out the grandmother, "I am too weak to get up from bed."

The wolf threw open the door, went straight to the grandmother's bed and ate her up. Then he put on her clothes and her bed cap, and lay in her bed.

Little Red Riding Hood gathered many flowers, and then slowly found her way back to the path and walked to her grandmother's. She was surprised to find the front door standing open and, when she went inside, she had a strange feeling and said to herself, *Oh dear! How uneasy I am here today.*

She called out, "Good morning," but there was no answer. She went over to the bed.

"Oh, Grandmother," she said, "what big ears you have!"

"All the better to hear you with, my dear," came the reply.

"But Grandmother, what big eyes you have!" said Little Red Riding Hood.

"All the better to see you with, my dear."

"Oh! But Grandmother, what a terrible big mouth you have!"

"All the better to *eat* you with, my dear!"

With one bound, the wolf leapt out of the bed and swallowed up Little Red Riding Hood!

Then, with his belly full, he lay down again, fell asleep and began to snore very loudly.

A huntsman, out shooting wolves, was just passing the house, and heard the snoring. He thought he would go inside and see whether the old woman needed anything. On the bed he saw the sleeping wolf.

He was about to shoot the wolf, when he stopped and wondered whether the grandmother might still be saved. He took a pair of scissors, and cut open the wolf's stomach. When he had made two snips, Little Red Riding Hood sprang out, crying, "I have been so frightened! It was so dark inside the wolf!" Her grandmother also came out alive, for the wolf had been in such a hurry, he had swallowed them whole.

Little Red Riding Hood fetched great stones to fill the wolf's belly. When he woke, the stones were so heavy that he collapsed at once, and fell dead.

They all rejoiced. The huntsman cut away the dead wolf's skin and took it home for a rug. Grandmother ate the cake Little Red Riding Hood had brought her and began to feel a little stronger. And Little Red Riding Hood thought to herself that she would never again talk to strangers or wander off the path in the wood.

12

The Town Musicians
of Bremen

There once was a donkey who had worked hard carrying corn sacks to the mill for many years, but whose strength was fading. These days he was struggling to keep up with his master's demands, and could see that his future looked bleak. His master would probably have him slaughtered once his feed cost more than he could earn. He decided to run away, and he set out for the town of Bremen.

In Bremen, he thought, *I could be a town musician.*

When he had walked some distance, he found a hound lying on the road, panting as though he had run a long way.

"Why are you panting, big fellow?" asked the donkey.

"I have run away," replied the hound. "I am getting older and weaker, and can no longer hunt, so my master wanted to kill me. But how will I earn my food?"

"I tell you what," said the donkey, "I am going to Bremen, to be a town musician there. You could come with me; I will play the lute, and you could beat the kettledrum."

The hound agreed, and on they went.

Before long they came to a cat, sitting on the path, with a face like three rainy days.

"Now then, old pussycat, what has gone wrong for you?" asked the donkey.

"Who can be merry when their life is in danger?" answered the cat. "Because I am now getting old, and my teeth are worn to stumps, and I prefer to sit by the fire rather than hunt mice, my mistress wanted to drown me. I ran away, but now where am I to go?"

"Come with us to Bremen. We will be town musicians!"

The cat thought it was a good plan, and went with them. After walking a distance, the three fugitives came to a farmyard, where a cockerel was sitting on the gate, crowing with all his might.

"What is the matter?" asked the donkey.

"Guests are coming on Sunday, and the farmer's wife has no pity. She has told the cook she intends to eat me in the soup, and this evening I am to have my head cut off! I am crowing while still I can."

"Cockerel," said the donkey, "you had better come away with us. We are going to Bremen. You can always find something better than death. You have a good voice, and we can make music together!"

The cockerel agreed to this plan, and all four went on side-by-side. They could not reach the city of Bremen in one day, however, and night was coming on. The cockerel flew high into a tree and saw a light burning further up the road. They decided to go towards it and see whether they could find shelter.

They came to a well-lit house.

Because he was biggest, the donkey went to the window and looked in.

"What do you see?" asked the cockerel.

"What do I see?" answered the donkey. "A table covered with good things to eat and drink, and a band of robbers sitting at it enjoying themselves."

"That's just what *we* need!" said the cockerel.

"Yes, yes! Ah, if only it were us in there!" said the donkey.

Then, together, the animals came up with a plan for driving away the robbers. The donkey placed his forefeet upon the window ledge, the hound jumped on his back, the cat climbed on the dog, and lastly the cockrel flew up and perched on the head of the cat.

They began to perform their music: the donkey brayed, the hound barked, the cat mewed, and the cockerel crowed. Then they burst through the window into the room, shattering the glass!

At this horrible din, the robbers sprang up, thinking that a ghost had come in, and they fled to the forest in great fright. The four companions now sat down at the table, and ate all they could wish for.

As soon as the four musicians were finished, they put out the light and each found a suitable sleeping place. The donkey lay on some straw in the yard, the hound rested behind the door, the cat curled up on the warm hearth, and the cockerel perched on a roof beam. They were tired from their long walk, and soon went to sleep.

When it was past midnight, and the robbers saw all was dark and quiet in the house, the captain ordered one of them to go inside and and look about.

This robber found all was still. He went into the dark kitchen to light a candle, and, thinking the glistening fiery eyes of the cat were live coals, he held a match to them to light it. The cat did not understand, and flew in his face, spitting and scratching. The robber was dreadfully frightened, and ran to the back door, but the dog, who lay there, sprang up and bit his leg; and as he ran across the dark yard by the dunghill, the donkey gave him a smart kick with its hind foot. The cockerel, too, who had been awakened by the noise, cried down from the beam, "Cock-a-doodle-doo!"

The robber ran back as fast as he could to his captain, and said, "There is a horrible witch sitting in the house, who spat on me and scratched my face with her long claws. And by the door stands a man with a knife, who stabbed me in the leg. And in the yard there lies a black monster, who beat me with a wooden club. And above, upon the roof, sits the judge, who called out, 'Bring me the robber, do!' so I got away as well as I could."

After this the robbers never again dared enter the house; but it suited the four musicians of Bremen so well that they never wanted to leave.

13

Puss in Boots

There was once a miller who had three sons, a mill, a donkey and a tomcat. The sons worked in the mill. The donkey carried corn to the mill and flour from the mill, and the cat chased the mice.

Then the miller died and the eldest son inherited the mill, the second son inherited the donkey and the youngest inherited the cat. This last son was very downcast about his lot and said to himself, "My eldest brother can work the mill, my other brother at least has a donkey to ride on and to carry things, but what on earth can I do with a cat? Once I have skinned him and made a pair of gloves out of his pelt, that will be all I gain."

The cat heard every word the miller's son said, and he spoke back to him. "Listen," he said, "it won't do you much good to kill me and make a pair of poor gloves out of my pelt. Instead, have a pair of boots made for me so that I can look respectable, and I'll soon be of some use to you."

The miller's son was very surprised to hear the cat speaking, but just then the shoemaker happened to be passing, so he called him in and got him to make a pair of boots for the cat. As soon as the boots were ready, the cat put them on, took a sack and put some corn into it. He slung the sack over his shoulder and marched off on his two hind legs.

Now at that time, the land was ruled by a King who was excessively fond of partridge pie, but, alas, there was a shortage of partridges. The forest was full of them, but the birds were so cunning that no huntsman could get near them. But the cat reckoned he could do better than the huntsmen. When he reached the wood he opened the mouth of the sack, spread the corn about inside the sack, and laid the long end of the sack's cord through the grass and under a fence. Then he hid and kept a sharp lookout. Very soon the partridges came along, saw the corn inside the sack and one after the other they hopped inside. The cunning cat pulled the cord, closing the mouth of the sack, and, lifting the whole lot onto his shoulder, off he went, straight to the King's palace.

At the gate the sergeant of the guard decided a cat in boots might amuse the King. Before the throne, the cat bowed deeply and said, "I come from my master, Count Alas de Molino, who sends you this present." Then he opened the sack and showed the King the partridges.

The King was delighted and ordered the royal treasurer to fill the cat's sack with gold, saying, "Take this back to your master and thank him for his gift."

Meanwhile, the poor miller's son was back at home sitting by the window with his head in his hands, thinking about how he had given his last penny to have some boots made for his cat, when what good could that bring him? But then the cat came in, opened up his sack, and emptied out the gold in front of the astonished lad.

"There, you've got something for the boots you had made for me. Best greetings from the King who thanks you very much."

The lad rejoiced at his new wealth, wondering how it had come about, so the cat took off his boots and told him the story. "Now you have got enough money, but it won't stop there. Tomorrow I shall put my boots on again and you will be even richer. I have told the King that you are a count."

Next morning the cat went off again in his boots. He again brought the King a good bagful of partridges. This went on every day, and every day the cat brought home gold in the sack. The King grew very fond of him, and he was allowed to wander about the palace.

One day the cat was standing in the palace kitchen, warming himself by the fire, when the coachman came in swearing, "I wish the King and the princess would go hang themselves. I was just about to go and enjoy myself in the inn, drinking and playing cards, but now I'm told I have to take them for a drive in the carriage to the lake."

As soon as the cat heard that, he went straight home and said to his master, "If you would like to be a rich count, come with me to the lake and go bathing in it."

The miller's son could not imagine how bathing might lead to riches, but he followed the cat. By the lake he took off all his clothes and jumped into the water. The cat quietly took the lad's clothes and hid them.

Almost immediately, the King came along in his carriage. Then the cat began to wail loudly and called to the King, "Oh, your gracious majesty, help! My master, the Count Alas de Molino, was bathing here in the lake, but a thief came and stole all his clothes, which were lying on the bank.

Now my lord count is in the water and dare not come out, and if he stays in much longer he will catch his death of cold."

When the King heard this he ordered his carriage to stop and one of the footmen had to ride back to the palace at full speed and bring a suit of clothes. These were then given to the miller's son, who put them on, and the King invited him to ride in the carriage, for he was delighted to meet the count who had given him all those fat partridges. The princess was also very cheerful because the count was young and handsome and pleased her very much. And so they drove on happily.

But the cat had run on ahead. He came to a huge meadow where more than a hundred people were making hay.

"Who does this meadow belong to?" asked the cat.

"To the great magician."

"Listen, very soon the King will come past, and when he asks who owns the meadow, answer 'Count Alas de Molino'. Say it, or be killed."

Then the cat went on further until he came to a cornfield that was so big you could not see from one end to the other, and there were more than two hundred people cutting corn.

"Who does this cornfield belong to?" asked the cat.

"To the great magician."

"When the King comes past, tell him that it belongs to Count Alas de Molino, otherwise you will all be killed."

Finally the cat came to a magnificent wood where more than three hundred people were felling great oak trees. Once again the cat ordered the people on pain of death to tell the King that the wood belonged to the count.

Now all the people were greatly awed by the cat because of his boots, and decided wisely to do as he had told them.

Soon after, the cat came to the magician's castle, went boldly inside and found the magician, who looked at him with contempt. But the cat bowed low and said, "I have heard that you are able to change yourself into any animal you wish. I can believe that you can turn yourself into a fox or a wolf, but I can hardly believe that you can turn yourself into an elephant, so I have come to see if this is really true."

The magician said, "It's true!" and there he stood: a huge elephant in front of the cat. Then the cat asked him whether he could turn himself into a lion, and he did.

Finally the cat said, "That was wonderful, and I am now sure that you are the greatest magician in the world, but I still cannot believe that it is possible for you to turn your great self into a tiny animal, such as a mouse."

The magician was flattered by the cat's words and said, "Of course I can," and he turned himself into a tiny mouse. The cat immediately pounced on the mouse and ate him up, and that was the end of the magician.

Meantime, the King was driving along with the count and the princess. Soon they came to the meadow and the King asked, "Who does all that hay belong to?"

"To Count Alas de Molino," the haymakers all replied.

"Sir Count, you have a fine piece of land there," said the King.

Then they came to the cornfield.

"Whose is all that corn?" asked the King.

"It belongs to Count Alas de Molino," said the corn cutters.

"Marvellous land you have, Sir Count."

When they came to the wood, the King asked once more, and again was told that the wood belonged to the count.

"Sir Count, you must be a wealthy man, I don't believe my forest is half as fine."

Finally they came to the magician's castle, and there was the cat, standing at the top of the steps to welcome them. When the carriage came to a halt the cat sprang down and opened the door and said, "Your majesty, you have now come to the castle of my master, Count Alas de Molino, and your visit will do him great honour."

The King stepped out of the carriage and admired the splendid building that seemed to him more magnificent than his own palace. The count led the princess up the steps and into the great hall, which sparkled with gold and gems. And there the princess was engaged to marry the young man.

So it came about that, after the death of the King, the miller's son became King. And Puss in Boots became the prime minister.

14

Sleeping Beauty

A long time ago there was a King and Queen who said every day in vain, "If only we had a child!" Then at long last the Queen gave birth to a baby girl who was so pretty that the King could not contain his joy and ordered a great feast. He invited his family, friends and acquaintances, and also the Wise Women, so that they would take a kind interest in the child. There were thirteen Wise Women in his kingdom, but he only had twelve golden plates for them to eat off, so one of them was not invited.

The feast was very grand. When it came to an end, each Wise Woman bestowed a magic gift upon the baby: one gave virtue, another beauty, a third riches, and so on, until the princess had been promised everything in the world that one can wish for.

When eleven of the Wise Women had made their promises, suddenly the thirteenth came in. She was furious and vengeful because she had not been invited to the feast. Without greeting or even looking at anyone, she cried out, "The King's daughter shall, in her fifteenth year, prick herself with a spindle, and fall down dead." Then she turned and left.

Everyone was shocked, but the twelfth Wise Woman, whose good wish was still unspoken, came forward. She could not undo the evil promise, but she could soften it. She said, "The princess shall not fall down dead, but into a deep sleep for a hundred years. Then she can be woken by a King's son."

The King tried everything to keep his dear child from the promised misfortune. He gave orders that every spindle in the whole kingdom should be burnt. Meanwhile the gifts of the first eleven Wise Women were fulfilled and the young girl became every day more beautiful, modest, good natured and wise.

It happened that on the very day when she turned fifteen years old, the King and Queen were not at home, so the princess was left alone in the castle. She wandered around into all sorts of places, looked into rooms and bedchambers just as she liked, and at last came to an old tower. She climbed up the narrow winding staircase and tried a little door at the top. There in a small room sat an old woman with a spindle, busily spinning her flax.

"Good day, what is it that you are doing?" asked the King's daughter, for of course she had never seen a spindle or the work of spinning flax into thread.

"I am spinning," said the old woman, and nodded her head.

"What is this thing, that rattles round so merrily?" asked the girl, reaching for the spindle. She had scarcely touched it when it pricked her finger and the magic spell was fulfilled. She fell down in a deep sleep.

This sleep extended over the whole castle: the King and Queen, who had just come home, fell asleep where they sat in the great hall, and the whole of the court slept with them.

The horses, too, went to sleep in the stable, the dogs in the yard, the pigeons upon the roof, the flies on the wall; even the fire that was flaming on the hearth became quiet and slept, and the cook, who was just going to pull the hair of the scullery boy because he had forgotten something, let him go, and went to sleep.

A hedge of thorns grew up all around the castle until nothing could be seen, not even the flag on the roof.

After long, long years, a King's son came to that country, and heard an old man talking about the thorn hedge, and the stories of a castle that stood behind it, in which a beautiful princess had been asleep for a hundred years. The young prince longed to know whether there was any truth in this tale, and to see the fabled castle and the beautiful princess.

It happened that one hundred years had now passed since the princess fell asleep, so when the King's son approached the thorn hedge, he found it consisted only of large and lovely flowers, which parted and let him pass unhurt, then closed again behind him.

He found the castle. In the yard he saw the horses and hounds lying asleep; on the roof sat the pigeons with their heads under their wings. When he entered, the flies were asleep upon the wall, and the maid was slumbering by a black hen she had been going to pluck. In the great hall he saw the whole of the court sleeping, and up by the throne lay the King and Queen.

At last he came to the tower, and opened the door into the little room where the princess was asleep. There she lay, so beautiful that he could not turn his eyes away; he bent down and kissed her. The princess awoke, and looked at him sweetly.

They went down together, and the King woke, and the Queen, and the whole court, and they all looked at each other in great astonishment. The horses in the stable stood up and shook themselves; the hounds jumped up and wagged their tails; the pigeons on the roof lifted their heads from under their wings, looked round, and flew into the sky; the flies on the wall crept again; the fire in the kitchen burnt up and flickered; the cook hit the boy around the head; and the maid finished plucking the black hen.

The marriage of the King's son and the princess was celebrated with great splendour, and they lived contented to the end of their days.

15

Snow White and the Seven Dwarfs

Once upon a time in the middle of winter, when flakes of snow were falling like feathers from the sky, a Queen sat at a window sewing. The frame of the window was made of black ebony, and while she was sewing, she pricked her finger with the needle, and three drops of blood fell upon the snow. The red looked pretty on the white snow, and she thought to herself, "How I would love to have a child as white as snow, as red as blood, and as black as this window frame."

Soon after, she had a little daughter, whose skin was white as snow, lips were as red as blood, and hair was as black as ebony. The baby girl was called Snow White.

The Queen died, and, after a year had passed, the King married another wife. She was a beautiful woman, but proud and haughty, and she could not bear to be less beautiful than anyone else. She had a wonderful looking glass: when she stood in front of it and said,

> Mirror, mirror, on the wall,
> Who in this land is the fairest of all?

the looking glass would answer,

> You, Queen, are the fairest of all!

Then she was satisfied, for she knew that the looking glass always spoke the truth.

But Snow White was growing up, and becoming ever more beautiful. By the time she was fourteen years old, she was as beautiful as the day, and more beautiful than the Queen herself. So when the Queen asked her looking glass,

> Mirror, mirror, on the wall,
> Who in this land is the fairest of all?

it answered,

> Lady Queen, you are fair and bright,
> But more fair still is young Snow White.

Then the Queen was shocked, and turned yellow and green with envy. From that hour, whenever she looked at Snow White her heart heaved in her chest because she hated the girl so much.

The envy and pride grew in her heart like a weed, so that she had no peace, day or night. She called a huntsman, and said, "Take the child away into the forest. I will no longer have her in my sight. Kill her, and bring me back her lung and liver as proof."

The huntsman took Snow White away, but when he had drawn his knife, she began to weep, and said, "Dear huntsman, do not take my life! I will run away into the wild forest, and never come home again."

She was so beautiful, the huntsman took pity on her and said, "Run away, then, you poor girl..." *The wild beasts will soon have devoured you*, he thought sadly. He killed a young boar and cut out its lung and liver to take to the Queen.

The poor child was all alone in the great forest, and terrified. Then she began to run; she ran over sharp stones and through thorns, and the wild beasts ran past her, but did her no harm.

She ran as far as her feet would go, then she saw a little cottage and went in to rest. Everything in the cottage was small, but neat and clean. There was a table with a white cloth, and seven little plates, and seven little mugs. Against the wall stood seven little beds side-by-side.

Snow White was so hungry and thirsty that she ate some vegetables and bread from each plate and drank a drop of wine out of each mug, for she did not wish to take everything from only one person. Then, as she was so tired, she lay down on one of the little beds, and went to sleep.

When it was dark, the owners of the cottage came back. They were seven dwarfs who dug for precious metals in the mountains. They lit their seven candles, and saw that someone had been there, eating from their plates and drinking from their mugs. Who could it be?

Then the seventh dwarf looked at his bed and saw Snow White, lying there asleep. They all cried out with astonishment, and brought their seven little candles so the light fell on her face. "Oh, heavens! Oh, heavens!" they cried, "What a lovely girl!" and they did not wake her, but let her sleep on in the bed.

When it was morning, Snow White woke up and was frightened when she saw the seven dwarfs. But they were friendly and asked her what her name was.

"My name is Snow White," she answered.

"How have you come to our house?" asked the dwarfs.

She told them that her stepmother had wished to have her killed, but that the huntsman had spared her life, and that she had run for the whole day, until at last she had found their cottage.

The dwarfs said, "If you will take care of our house, cook, make the beds, wash, sew, and knit, and if you will keep everything neat and clean, you can stay with us and you shall want for nothing."

"Yes," said Snow White, "with all my heart," and she stayed with them. During the days they went to the mountains looking for copper and gold, and she kept the house in order and made supper.

Snow White was alone the whole day, so the good dwarfs warned her, "Beware of your stepmother, she will soon know that you are here. Be sure to let no one come in."

The Queen believed that Snow White was dead, so she thought she must again be the most beautiful of all. She went to her looking glass and said,

> Mirror, mirror, on the wall,
> Who in this land is the fairest of all?

The looking glass answered,

> Oh, Queen, you are fairest of all I see,
> But over the hills, where the seven dwarfs dwell,
> Snow White is still alive and well,
> And none is so fair as she.

Then the wicked Queen was astounded, for she knew that the looking glass never lied, so the huntsman must have betrayed her, and Snow White must still live.

Envy let her have no rest. She thought of nothing but how she might kill her stepdaughter.

She disguised herself as an old peddler woman and painted her face so that no one could recognise her. She

went over the mountains to the seven dwarfs' cottage, knocked at the door and cried, "Pretty things to sell, very cheap, very cheap."

Snow White looked out of the window and answered, "Good day, my good woman, what have you to sell?"

"Pretty things," said the disguised Queen, "ribbons and laces of all colours." Snow White unbolted the door and bought a pretty lace. "What a mess you look," said the old woman. "Come, I will lace your corset properly."

Snow White had no suspicions, and stood still while her new lace was threaded. But the old woman tightened the lace so quickly that Snow White lost her breath and fell down as if dead.

Now I am the most beautiful, said the Queen to herself, and ran away.

In the evening, the seven dwarfs came home, and were shocked when they saw their dear Snow White lying on the ground. They lifted her up, saw the tight laces and cut them. She began to breathe a little, and after a while she came to life again.

When the dwarfs heard what had happened, they said, "That old peddler woman was none other than the wicked Queen. Don't let anyone in when we are not with you."

When she reached home, the Queen went to her looking glass and asked,

> Mirror, mirror, on the wall,
> Who in this land is the fairest of all?

and it answered as before,

Oh, Queen, you are fairest of all I see,
But over the hills, where the seven dwarfs dwell,
Snow White is still alive and well,
And none is so fair as she.

When she heard that, the Queen's blood rushed to her heart with fear and anger; she saw plainly that Snow White was still alive. She could not rest until she had thought of a more deadly plan. She made a poisonous hair comb, then she disguised herself again, as a different old woman. She went over the mountains to the seven dwarfs' cottage, knocked at the door, and cried, "Good things to sell, cheap, cheap!"

Snow White looked out and said, "Go away. I cannot let anyone come in."

"Well, you can look," said the old woman, and held out the poisonous comb. Snow White thought the comb was so pretty, she was quite distracted by it and opened the door. She bought the comb and the old woman said, "I will put it in your hair for you." Snow White let the old woman do as she pleased, but as soon as the comb touched her, the poison took effect, and she fell down senseless.

"You paragon of beauty," said the wicked woman, "you are finished now," and she went away.

Fortunately it was almost evening, and the seven dwarfs came home. When they saw Snow White lying on the ground as if dead, they at once suspected the step-mother. They looked for what might have hurt her, and found the poisoned comb. When they took it out of her hair, Snow White came to herself, and told them what had happened. Then they warned her once more to keep the door closed.

The Queen, at home, went to the looking glass and said,

Mirror, mirror, on the wall,
Who in this land is the fairest of all?

It answered as before,

Oh, Queen, you are fairest of all I see,
But over the hills, where the seven dwarfs dwell,
Snow White is still alive and well,
And none is so fair as she.

When she heard this, the wicked woman shook with rage. "Snow White shall die," she cried, "even if it costs me my life!"

In a lonely room, she made a poisonous apple. On the outside it looked delicious: shiny and white, with a red cheek, so that anyone who saw it would long for it. But eating a piece of it meant certain death.

She painted her face and dressed herself like a farmer's wife then she knocked at the dwarfs' cottage door. Snow White put her head out the window and said, "I'm sorry, I cannot let anyone in. The seven dwarfs have forbidden me."

"It doesn't matter, I will soon sell my bags of beautiful apples to others," said the old woman. "Here, I will give you one."

"No," said Snow White, "I dare not take anything."

"Are you afraid of poison?" said the old woman. "Look, I will cut the apple in two. You eat the red cheek, and I will eat the white." The apple was made so deviously that only the red cheek was poisoned. Snow White longed for the delicious-looking fruit, and when she saw that the woman

ate part of it, she could resist no longer. She stretched out her hand and took the poisonous red piece. As soon as she bit into it, she fell down dead.

Then the Queen looked at her with a dreadful face, and said, "White as snow, red as blood, black as ebony! This time the dwarfs cannot wake you up again."

And when, at home, she asked her looking glass,

> Mirror, mirror, on the wall,
> Who in this land is the fairest of all?

it answered at last,

> Oh, Queen, in this land you are fairest of all.

Then her envious heart had rest, so far as an envious heart can have rest.

When the dwarfs came home in the evening, they found Snow White lying on the floor, dead. They looked for anything poisonous, unlaced her, washed her, but it was all of no use, the poor girl remained dead. They laid her in a glass coffin, and all seven of them sat around it and wept for her, for three long days. They put the coffin out upon the mountain, and one of them always stayed by it and watched it. Birds came too, and wept for Snow White; first an owl, then a raven, and last a dove.

Snow White lay a long, long time in the coffin, and she did not change. She looked as if she were asleep, for her skin was still as white as snow, her lips as red as blood, and her hair as black as ebony.

It happened one day that a King's son came to the mountain and saw the coffin and the beautiful Snow White inside it. He said to the dwarfs, "Let me have the coffin, I will give you whatever you want for it."

But the dwarfs answered, "We will not part with it for all the gold in the world."

Then he said, "Let me have it as a gift, for I cannot live without seeing Snow White. I will honour and prize her as my dearest possession." Then the good dwarfs trusted him and took pity on him, and gave him the coffin.

The King's son had it carried away by his servants, but as they went they stumbled over a tree stump and jolted the coffin. The poisonous piece of apple flew out of Snow White's throat. She opened her eyes, lifted up the lid of the coffin, sat up, and was alive once more. "Oh, heavens, where am I?" she cried.

The King's son, full of joy, said, "You are with me," and told her what had happened. He said, "I love you more than everything in the world, come and marry me."

Snow White said yes, and went with him, and their wedding was held with great show and splendour.

But Snow White's wicked stepmother was invited to the feast. When she had dressed herself in beautiful clothes, she went to the looking glass, and said,

> Mirror, mirror, on the wall,
> Who in this land is the fairest of all?

The glass answered,

> Oh, Queen, of all here the fairest you are,
> But young yonder Queen is fairer by far.

Then the wicked woman uttered a curse, and was so utterly wretched that she didn't know what to do. At first she would not go to the wedding at all, but then she had to see the young Queen. When she went in, she recognised Snow White, and stood still with rage and fear. But iron slippers had already been placed on the fire. They were brought in with tongs, and set before her. Then she was forced to put on the red-hot shoes, and dance until she dropped down dead.

16

Rumpelstiltskin

O nce there was a miller who was poor, but who had a beautiful daughter. Now it happened that he had to go and speak to the King and, in order to seem important, he foolishly said, "I have a daughter who can spin straw into gold."

The King said to the miller, "This is an art that pleases me well. If your daughter is as clever as you say, bring her tomorrow to my palace, and I will put her to the test."

When the girl was brought to him the next day, the King took her into a room full of straw, gave her a spinning wheel and a reel, and said, "Now, set to work, and if by tomorrow morning you have not spun this straw into gold, you must die."

He locked up the room, and left her there. The poor miller's daughter did not know what to do; she had no idea how straw could be spun into gold. She grew more and more frightened, and began to weep.

But all at once the door opened, and in came a little man, who said, "Good evening, Miss Miller. Why are you crying so?"

"Alas!" answered the girl, "I have to spin straw into gold, and I do not know how to do it."

"What will you give me," said the little man, "if I do it for you?"

"My necklace," said the girl. The little man took the necklace, seated himself in front of the wheel, and whirr, whirr, whirr, three turns and the reel was full. Then he put another reel on, and whirr, whirr, whirr, three times round, and the second was full too. And so it went on until the morning, when all the straw was spun, and all the reels were full of gold.

At daybreak, the King came into the room, and when he saw the gold he was astonished and delighted, but his heart became greedier. He had the miller's daughter taken into another, much larger room full of straw, and commanded her to also spin that into gold in one night, or she would be killed.

The girl did not know how to save herself, and was crying, when the door opened again, and the little man appeared. He said, "What will you give me if I spin that straw into gold for you?"

"The ring on my finger," answered the girl. The little man took the ring, again began to turn the wheel, and by morning had spun all the straw into glittering gold.

The King rejoiced beyond measure at the sight, but still he was not satisfied. He had the miller's daughter taken to a still larger room full of straw, and said, "You must spin this, too, in the course of the night. But if you succeed, you shall be my wife."

Even if she is a poor miller's daughter, he thought, *I could not find a richer wife in the whole world.*

When the girl was alone, the little man came a third time, and said, "What will you give me if I spin the straw for you this time?"

"I have nothing left to give," answered the girl.

"Then promise me that if you become Queen, you will give me your first child."

Who knows whether that will ever happen? thought the miller's daughter; and, not knowing how else to escape the King's threat, she promised the little man what he wanted, and he once more spun the straw into gold.

When the King came in the morning, and found another room full of riches as he had wished, they were married, and the pretty miller's daughter became Queen.

A year later, the new young Queen had a beautiful baby, and she never gave a thought to the little man who spun straw into gold. But one day he suddenly came into her room, and said, "Now, give me what you promised."

The Queen was horror-struck, and offered him all the riches of the kingdom if he would leave her the child. But he said, "No, something alive is dearer to me than all the treasures in the world."

Then the Queen began to lament and cry, and the little man felt some pity for her. "I will give you three days," said he. "If in that time you find out my name, then you shall keep your child."

So the Queen thought the whole night of all the names she had ever heard, and she sent a messenger over the country to inquire, far and wide, for any other names that there might be. When the little man came the next day, she began with Caspar, Melchior, Balthazar, and said all the names she knew, one after another. But to every one the little man said, "That is not my name."

On the second day she sent her servants to inquire the names of all the people in the region, and she repeated to the little man the most uncommon and curious ones she

heard. "Perhaps your name is Shortribs, or Sheepshanks, or Laceleg?"

But he always answered, "That is not my name."

On the third day, a messenger came back to the palace, and said, "I have not been able to find a single new name, but as I came to a high mountain at the end of the forest, I saw a little house, and in front of the house a fire was burning, and round the fire a ridiculous little man was jumping. He hopped on one leg, and shouted,

> The Queen's child will be mine no less,
> They will inquire and hunt in vain,
> For nobody could ever guess,
> That Rumpelstiltskin is my name!

You may imagine how glad the Queen was to learn this!

Soon afterwards the little man came in, and asked, "Now, Mistress Queen, what is my name?"

At first she said, "Is your name Conrad?"

"No, that is not my name."

"Is your name Harry?"

"That is not my name."

"Perhaps your name is ... Rumpelstiltskin?"

"What evil being told you that name?" cried the little man. In his anger he stamped his right foot so hard that his whole leg went deep into the ground, then in rage he pulled at his left leg so hard with both hands that he tore himself in two.

17

The Two Brothers

Once upon a time there were two brothers, one rich and the other poor. The rich one was a goldsmith and black at heart. The poor one was a broom-maker and was good and honourable. The poor one had twin sons, who were as like each other as two drops of water. The twin boys often dropped by their rich uncle's house, and got some scraps to eat.

One day, when the poor man was going into the forest to fetch brushwood, he saw a golden bird that was more beautiful than any bird he had ever seen before. He picked up a small stone, threw it at the bird and managed to hit it, but only one golden feather fell down, and the bird flew away. The man took the feather to his rich brother, the goldsmith, who looked at it. "It is pure gold!" he said, and gave him a great deal of money for it.

Next day, the poor broom-maker climbed into a birch tree to cut a couple of branches, when the same bird flew out. He found a nest that had a golden egg lying inside it. He took the egg and showed it to his brother, who again said, "It is pure gold," and gave him what it was worth. The rich goldsmith said, "I would like to have the bird itself." So the poor brother went into the forest, and this time when he saw the golden bird he was able to throw a stone and bring it down. He carried it to his wealthy brother, who gave him a great heap of gold for it.

The goldsmith knew what kind of bird this was. He called his wife and said, "Roast me the golden bird, and take care that none of it is lost. I must eat it all myself." The bird was magical, so whoever ate its heart and liver would find a piece of gold beneath their pillow every morning. The woman made the bird ready, put it on the spit, and let it roast. But then when she stepped out of the kitchen, the broom-maker's twin sons ran in. They turned the spit once or twice and two bits of the bird fell into the dripping tin. One of the boys said, "Let's eat these little bits. I am so hungry, and no one will ever miss them."

They ate them, but the goldsmith's wife came back to the kitchen and saw that they were chewing. She realised they must have eaten the bird's heart and liver, and was frightened her husband would be angry. She quickly killed a young cock, took out its heart and liver, and put them beside the golden bird. When it was roasted, she carried it to the goldsmith, who ate it all himself, leaving nothing. Next morning, however, when he felt beneath his pillow, expecting to bring out a piece of gold, there were no more gold pieces than there had ever been.

When the two children woke up, something fell rattling to the ground and they found two gold pieces! They took them to their father, who was astonished. The next morning they found two more, and then again every day. The broom-maker went to his brother and told him of these coins strangely appearing. The goldsmith knew at once how it must have come about. He was envious and hard hearted and said to his brother, "Your children are in league with evil. Do not take the gold, and do not let them live in your house any longer, or the evil will invade you too." The broom-maker was frightened, so, painful as it was to him, he led the twins deep into the forest, and with a sad heart he left them there.

The twin brothers searched for the way home, but they just became more lost. At last they met a huntsman, who asked, "Who do you children belong to?"

"We are the poor broom-maker's sons," they replied, and they told him that their father would not keep them in the house any longer because a piece of gold lay under their pillows every morning.

"Come," said the huntsman, "that is not such a bad fate,

as long as you keep honest, and are not idle." He was a good man who liked children, and had none of his own, so he took them home with him and said, "I will be your father, and bring you up till you have grown enough not to need me." They learnt hunting from him, and he kept for them the pieces of gold that arrived each morning, in case they should need them in the future.

When the twins were grown up, the huntsman took them into the forest and said, "Today, if you make your trial shot, I can release you from your apprenticeship, and make you huntsmen." He pointed to a covey of wild geese flying in the form of a triangle, and said, "Shoot down one from each corner." Each of the boys accomplished this, and the huntsman said, "You are skilled huntsmen. Your apprenticeship is over."

The brothers thought together and then asked him, "We have now finished learning, but we must prove ourselves in the world. Allow us to go away and travel."

This pleased their foster father, who said, "You talk like brave men. What you ask for has always been my wish for you. Go, and your courage will be rewarded."

When they were setting out, the huntsmen presented each of them with a good gun and a dog, and their saved-up gold pieces. When saying goodbye, he gave them a bright knife, and said, "If you ever separate, stick this knife into a tree at the place where you part, and then if one of you returns to it, he will be able to see how his brother is faring. For the side of the knife which is turned in the direction the brother went will rust if he dies, but will remain bright as long as he is alive."

The two brothers walked on together through a great forest. After two days they had eaten everything from their hunting pouches. They said, "We must shoot something or we will go hungry," and they loaded their guns. When a hare came running towards them, they took aim, but the hare cried,

> Dear huntsmen, if you let me live,
> Two little ones to you I'll give.

It sprang into the thicket, and brought back two baby hares. But the little creatures played so merrily, and were so pretty, that the huntsmen could not find it in their hearts to kill them. So they kept them, and the little hares jumped along beside them as they walked.

Soon after this, a fox crept past. They were just going to shoot it, when it cried,

> Dear huntsman, if you let me live,
> Two little ones to you I'll give.

The fox, too, brought two little foxes, and the huntsmen did not want to kill them either, so, like the hares, they followed behind.

It wasn't long before a wolf strode out of the bushes. The huntsmen made ready to shoot it, but the wolf cried,

> Dear huntsman, if you let me live,
> Two little ones to you I'll give.

The huntsmen put the two little wolves beside the other baby animals, and they followed along too. Then a bear came, and to save its own life added two young bears to the twin brothers' procession.

Finally, a lion came, and tossed his mane, and he too swapped two cubs to keep his life. Now the twin huntsmen had two lions, two bears, two wolves, two foxes and two hares who followed them and served them. They were still hungry, but the crafty foxes knew where there was a village, and there the brothers exchanged their gold coins for food, for themselves and the animals. They travelled on like this, from village to village.

After they had travelled for many months, they had found no place where they could settle together, so they agreed to part and try their luck in the world independently. They divided the animals, so that each of them had a lion, a bear, a wolf, a fox, and a hare. They said goodbye, promised to love each other like brothers until death, and stuck the knife that their foster father had given them into a tree. Then one went east, and the other went west.

The twin who went west arrived with his animals in a town that was hung with black. A villager explained that the next day their King's only daughter was to die.

The wandering twin asked, "Is she very ill?"

"No," answered the villager, "she is vigorous and healthy, nevertheless she must die. Outside the town there is a high

hill. On it lives a dragon that must eat a beautiful girl every year, or he destroys the whole country. Now all the girls have been given to him; there is no longer anyone left but the King's daughter. She must be given to him, and it is to be done tomorrow."

The huntsman asked, "Why doesn't someone kill the dragon?"

"Many knights have tried it," replied the villager, "but it has cost all of them their lives. The King has promised that he who conquers the dragon will marry his daughter, and will govern the kingdom after his death."

The huntsman said nothing more to this, but the next morning he took his animals, and climbed the dragon's hill. A little church stood at the top of it, and on the altar stood three full cups, with the inscription, "Whoever empties the cups will become the strongest man on earth, and will be able to wield the sword buried at the door of the church." The huntsman drank from the cups, and became so strong his hand could quite easily wield the heavy sword he found there.

The hour came when the princess was to be delivered to the dragon. From afar she saw the huntsman on the hill and thought it was the dragon waiting for her. She did not want to go, but because the whole town would have been destroyed, she was forced to make the miserable journey. The King and courtiers returned home full of grief, but the King's marshal was told to stand and watch from a distance.

When the King's daughter got to the top of the hill, it was not the dragon who stood there, but the young huntsman, who comforted her, and said he would save her. He led her into the church, and locked her in. It was not long before the seven-headed dragon arrived, roaring. Seeing the huntsman, he was astonished and said, "Many knights have left their lives here, I shall soon make an end of you, too," and he breathed fire from his seven jaws. The fire was intended to light the dry grass, suffocating the huntsman in the heat and smoke, but his animals came running and trampled out the flames. The dragon rushed towards the huntsman, but he swung his sword until it sang through the air, and he struck off three of the seven heads. The dragon became furious, and rose up in the air, spitting flames over the huntsman, but the huntsman once more drew out his sword, and cut off another three heads. The monster became faint but was just able to rush at the huntsman. With his last strength, the huntsman only managed to slice its tail off. But his animals came running and tore what was left of the dragon to pieces.

When the fight was over, the huntsman unlocked the church. He found the King's daughter lying on the floor, as she had fainted with fear. He showed her the dragon all cut to pieces, and told her that she was saved. She rejoiced and said, "Now you will be my dearest husband." She took off her coral necklace, and made collars to reward all the huntsman's animals. She gave her handkerchief, embroidered with her name, to the huntsman. He went and cut the tongues from the dragon's seven heads, wrapped them in the handkerchief, and preserved them carefully.

The huntsman was so weary from the battle, he said to the princess, "We are both exhausted, let's rest for a while." She agreed, and the huntsman said to the lion, "You keep watch, so that no one surprises us in our sleep." The lion was also weary from the fight. He called to the bear and said, "Lie down near me, I must sleep a little. Wake me if anything comes." The bear was also tired, and called the

wolf saying, "I must sleep a little, but if anything comes, wake me." The wolf called the fox and said, "If anything comes, wake me." The fox told the hare to wake him, but the poor hare was tired too, and had no one whom he could call to keep watch. He fell asleep. So now the King's daughter, the huntsman, the lion, the bear, the wolf, the fox, and the hare were all sound asleep.

The marshal, who had been told by the King to watch from a distance, took courage when he did not see the dragon fly away with the princess. Now the hill was quiet, he climbed to the top. There lay the dragon hacked and hewn to pieces on the ground, and nearby were the King's daughter and a huntsman with his animals, and all of them were fast asleep. The marshal was wicked and godless. He took his sword, cut off the huntsman's head, seized the princess in his arms, and carried her down the hill. She woke and was terrified, and the marshal said he would kill her if she did not obey him and promise to say it was he who killed the dragon.

He took her to the King, who was overjoyed when he saw his dear child, alive. The marshal said, "I have killed the dragon, and saved the princess and the whole kingdom. I demand to marry her, as you promised."

The King said to the princess, "Is what he says true?"

"It must indeed be true," she answered, "but I will not consent to be married until a year and a day have passed." She hoped in that time to hear something of the dear huntsman.

The animals still lay sleeping beside their dead master on the dragon's hill. The hare woke first and roused the fox, and the fox the wolf, and the wolf the bear, and the bear the lion. And when the lion woke and saw that the princess was gone and his master was dead, he began to roar frightfully and cried, "Who has done that? Bear, why didn't you wake me?"

The bear asked the wolf, "Why didn't you wake me?" and the wolf asked the fox, and the fox asked the hare. The poor hare did not know what to say, and the blame rested with him.

They were all going to pounce on him, but he said, "Don't kill me, I know how we can bring our master to life again. There is a mountain where a root grows, which can cure every illness and any wound." They let him go and a day later he was back, with the root. The lion put the huntsman's head on his body again, and the hare placed the root by the wound, and immediately the two united together again. The huntsman's heart beat, and life came back. He woke, and was alarmed when he did not see the princess. He thought, *She must have crept away while I was sleeping, to get rid of me.*

The lion in his great haste had put his master's head on the wrong way round, but the huntsman didn't notice because of his unhappy thoughts about the King's daughter. Then at noon, when he went to eat something, he saw that his head was turned backwards and could not understand it. The lion explained that they had all slept, and his head had been cut off, but they had cured the wound with a magic root, and that in his haste he had held the head the wrong way, but that he would repair his mistake. Then he tore the huntsman's head off again, turned it round, and the hare healed it with the root.

The huntsman was sad at heart. He set off travelling again around the world.

It came to pass that precisely at the end of one year, he came back to the same town where he had saved the

King's daughter from the dragon. This time the town was brightly hung with red. He asked a villager what it meant. The villager replied, "Last year our King's daughter was delivered to the dragon, but the marshal fought it and killed it, and so tomorrow their wedding is to be celebrated. That is why the town is covered with red cloth today, for joy."

The huntsman stayed at an inn in the town. Next day when the wedding was to take place, he said to the innkeeper, "Do you believe, sir host, that today I shall eat bread from the King's own table?"

"Nay," answered the host, "I would bet a hundred pieces of gold that will not come true." The huntsman accepted the wager, and set against it a purse with just the same number of gold pieces.

Then he called the hare and said, "Go, my dear runner, and fetch me some of the bread the King is eating." The hare ran to the palace and under the chair of the King's daughter, and scratched at her foot. She peeped down, and knew the hare by the collar she'd made from her coral necklace. She picked him up, carried him into her chamber, and said, "Dear hare, what do you want?"

He answered, "My master, who killed the dragon, is here, and has sent me to ask for a loaf of bread just like the bread the King eats." Then the princess was full of joy and ordered the baker to bring a loaf like those eaten by the King. The hare got on his hind legs, took the loaf in his front paws and carried it to his master.

Then the huntsman said, "Behold, innkeeper, the hundred pieces of gold are mine." The innkeeper was astonished, but the huntsman went on to say, "Yes, sir host, I have the bread, but now I will likewise have some of the King's roast meat."

The host said, "I should indeed like to see that," but he would make no more wagers.

The huntsman called the fox and said, "My little fox, go and fetch me some roast meat, just like the King eats." The fox ran to the palace and seated himself under the King's daughter's chair, and she recognised him by his collar.

He said to her, "My master, who killed the dragon, is here, and has sent me. I am to ask for some roast meat like that the King is eating." Then she ordered the cook to prepare a roast joint like the King's. The fox took the dish, waved away the flies and carried it to his master.

"Behold, sir host," said the huntsman, "bread and meat are here but now I will also have proper vegetables with it, like those eaten by the King." Then he sent the wolf to fetch vegetables just like the King eats, and the princess arranged for the wolf to have the vegetables. Next the huntsman sent the bear to bring back some sweet pastry just like the King was eating, and then the lion to find wine just like that drunk by the King. The princess recognised each animal by its collar, and met all their requests.

Finally, the huntsman said, "Behold, sir host, here I have bread, meat, vegetables, sweet pastry and wine just like the King has, and now I will dine with my animals." They all ate and drank, and he was joyful, for he knew that the King's daughter still loved him. The innkeeper was astonished at all that had arrived, and glad he had made no further bets.

Now the King said to his daughter at the royal table, "What did all the wild animals want, which have been coming to you, and going in and out of my palace?"

She replied, "I may not tell you, but you would do well to send for the master of these animals." The King sent a servant to the inn, and invited the stranger to the palace.

The King went to meet the huntsman and led him in, and his animals followed. The King gave him a seat near himself and his daughter, and the marshal, as bridegroom, sat on the other side, but he didn't recognise the huntsman.

At this very moment, the seven heads of the dragon were brought in to impress the court. The King declared, "These seven heads were cut off the dragon by the marshal, which is why today he is marrying my daughter."

But the huntsman stood up, opened the seven dragon mouths, and said, "Where are the tongues?"

Then the marshal was terrified, and grew pale and didn't know what to answer. At length in his anguish he said, "Dragons have no tongues."

The huntsman said, "Liars ought to have no tongues, but a dragon's tongues are the prize of the one who slays it," and he unfolded the handkerchief he carried, and there lay all seven tongues. He put each tongue into the dragon mouth to which it belonged, and they fitted exactly. Then he took the handkerchief, on which the princess's name was embroidered, and showed it to her, and asked who she had given it to.

She replied, "To he who killed the dragon."

And then he called his animals, and took the collar off each of them and asked the princess who the jewels belonged to.

She answered, "I divided them among the animals who helped conquer the dragon."

Then the huntsman declared, "When I was resting, tired from the fight, the marshal came and cut off my head. Then he carried away the King's daughter, and claimed it was he who had killed the dragon, but he lied. I prove this with the tongues, the handkerchief, and the necklace collars." He told how his animals had healed him using a wonderful root.

The King asked his daughter, "Is it true that this man killed the dragon?"

She answered, "Yes, it is true. I can reveal the wicked deed of the marshal, now that it has come to light without my telling. He made me promise to be silent. This is why I made the condition that the marriage should be delayed for a year and a day." The King summoned twelve councillors to pronounce judgment on the marshal, and they sentenced him to be torn to pieces by four bulls.

Then the King gave his daughter to the huntsman, and named him his ruler over the whole kingdom. The wedding was celebrated with great joy. The young King invited his father, the broom-maker, and his foster father, the huntsman, and loaded them with treasures. The young King and Queen were thoroughly happy, and lived cheerfully together.

The young King was still a huntsman. He often went out hunting and the faithful animals accompanied him. There was a forest nearby that was reported to be haunted. The young King was riding past it when he saw a snow-white deer and said to his servants, "Wait here until I return, I must chase that beautiful creature," and disappeared into the forest after it, followed only by his animals. His servants waited until evening, then they rode home and told the young Queen that the young King had followed a white hart and disappeared into the enchanted forest.

The young King kept getting near enough to the deer to take aim, only to have it bound away into the far distance. Eventually, it vanished altogether and he was lost, deep in the forest with night falling. He lit a fire near a tree, but then heard a groan from above. When he looked up, there was an old woman sitting in the tree, saying, "Oh, oh, oh, how cold I am!"

"Come down, and warm yourself," he said.

But she said, "No, your animals will bite me."

He answered, "They will do you no harm, old woman, do come down."

But the old woman was really a witch and she said, "I will throw down a wand from the tree, and if you strike them on the back with it, they will do me no harm." He touched his animals with her wand and they were instantly turned into stone. Now that the witch was safe from the animals, she leapt down and touched the young King with the wand too, turning him to stone. Then she laughed, and dragged him and the animals into a vault, where many more such stones already lay.

When the young King still did not come back, the young Queen became more and more worried.

It so happened that at this very time the young King's twin brother came into the kingdom. He had not settled, but had travelled here and there with his animals. Then it occurred to him to go and look at the knife in the trunk of the tree so he might learn how his twin brother was. His brother's side of the knife was half rusted and half bright. He thought, *A great misfortune must have befallen my brother, but perhaps I can still save him, for half the knife is still bright.*

He and his animals travelled in his brother's direction, and when he reached the town gate, a guard came to meet him, and asked, "Shall I announce you to the young Queen, for she has spent days in the greatest sorrow, afraid you were killed in the enchanted forest?" The twin realised that the guard thought he was his brother, who must be a young King, and he thought, *If I pass myself off as him, I will fit in here and then perhaps I can rescue him more easily.* So he allowed the guard to escort him to the castle, where he was received with great joy.

The young Queen thought this was her husband, and asked him why he had stayed away so long. He said he had not been able to find his way out of the forest.

At night he was taken to the royal bed, but he laid a two-edged sword between the young Queen and himself. She didn't know what this meant, but did not dare to ask.

He remained in the palace for two days, and asked about everything relating to the enchanted forest. At last he said, "I must hunt there once more." The young Queen and her father, the King, tried to persuade him not to, but he was determined. When he got to the forest, he had the same experience as his brother. He saw a snow-white deer and said to his hunting companions, "Stay here and wait until I return; I must chase that lovely beast." But he could not overtake the deer, and got so deep into the forest that he was forced to pass the night there. He lit a fire, and heard someone above him groaning about the cold. Looking up he saw the witch and invited her to warm herself down by the fire. She asked him to touch his animals with her wand so she needn't fear them, but with this request he realised she must be a witch. He tried to shoot, but lead bullets could not harm her. She laughed and cried out, "You cannot hit me."

At this, the huntsman tore three silver buttons off his coat, and loaded his gun with them. Her magic was useless against the silver, and she fell to the ground with a scream. He set his foot on her and said, "Old witch, if you do not instantly confess where my brother is, I will seize you with both my hands and throw you into the fire."

The witch was frightened and said, "He and his animals lie in a vault, turned to stone."

The twin brother forced her to bring all the stones in the vault back to life again. There stood the young King with his animals, and many others arose too: merchants, artisans and shepherds. They thanked the twin brother for saving them, and went to their homes.

When the brothers saw each other again, they embraced and rejoiced with all their hearts. They threw the witch on the fire, and with her death the forest opened up to be light and clear, and the King's palace could be seen in the distance, only a three-hour walk away.

The two brothers headed there together, and on the way they told each other their stories. The young King explained that he was ruler of the whole country, and his brother observed, "Yes, I saw this. When I went to the town, they all thought I was you. All royal honours were paid to me, the young Queen looked on me as her husband, and I had to eat at her side, and sleep in your bed." When the other heard that, he became so jealous and angry that he drew his sword, and struck off his brother's head. But when he saw him lying there dead, he was deeply sorry. "My brother saved me," he cried, "and I have killed him for it," and he wailed aloud. Then his hare offered to bring some of the root of life. He bounded off and fetched it while there was still time, and the dead man was brought to life again.

The twin brothers and their animals entered the palace together. The King said to his daughter, "Each of them looks exactly like the other! Say which is your husband, for I cannot tell."

Then she was in great distress, because she could not tell, but at last she remembered the collars she had given to the animals. She found the golden clasp on the lion, and cried in delight, "He who is followed by this lion is my true husband."

The young King laughed and said, "Yes, I am the right one!" They sat down together and ate, drank, and were merry.

That night when the young King came to bed, his wife said, "Why did you lay the two-edged sword between us these last nights? I thought you were going to kill me." So the young King knew how true his twin brother had been.

18

The Golden Goose

There were once three brothers, the youngest of whom was called Dummling, or Simpleton, and he was despised, mocked, and sneered at on every occasion. One day the eldest brother was going to the forest to chop wood. His mother gave him a beautiful sweet cake and a bottle of wine so he wouldn't be hungry or thirsty.

When he entered the forest, he met a little grey-haired old man, who said, "Do give me a piece of cake out of your pocket, and let me have a draught of your wine. I am so hungry and thirsty."

The clever eldest brother answered, "If I give you my cake and wine, I'll have none for myself. Be off with you." He left the little man standing and went on.

But when he began to chop down a tree, he made an awkward stroke and the axe cut him in the arm, so that he had to go home and have it bound up. This was the little grey man's doing.

Then the second son went into the forest, and his mother gave him, like the eldest, a cake and a bottle of wine. The little old grey man met him, and asked him for a piece of cake and a drink of wine. But the second son also said, sensibly enough, "What I give you will be taken away from my own lunch. Be off!" and he left the little man standing and went on. His punishment, however, came swiftly: when he had made a few blows at the tree he struck himself in the leg, and had to be carried home.

Then Dummling said, "Father, do let me go and cut wood."

The father answered, "Your brothers have hurt themselves trying. Don't go, you do not understand anything about it." But Dummling begged so long that at last he said, "Just go then, you will get wiser by hurting yourself."

His mother gave him a cake made with water and baked in the cinders, and a bottle of sour beer. When he came to the forest, the little old grey man met him, and said, "Give me a piece of your cake and a drink out of your bottle. I am so hungry and thirsty."

Dummling answered, "I have only cinder cake and sour beer. If that pleases you, we will sit down together and eat." So they sat down, but when Dummling pulled out his cinder cake, it was a fine sweet cake, and the sour beer had become good wine.

They ate and drank, and after that the little man said, "Since you have a good heart, and are willing to share what you have, I will give you good luck. There stands an old tree. Cut it down, and you will find something at the roots." Then the little man said goodbye.

Dummling cut down the tree, and when it fell there was a goose sitting in the roots with feathers of pure gold.

Dummling carried the golden goose to an inn where he was going to stay the night. The innkeeper had three daughters, who all saw the goose and wanted to pluck one of its golden feathers.

As soon as Dummling had gone up to his room to sleep, the eldest daughter seized the goose by the wing, but her finger and hand stuck fast to it.

The second daughter reached out too, but her hand touched her sister, and she was stuck fast as well.

The two stuck sisters screamed to the third to keep away, but this youngest thought, *The others are there, I may as well be there too*, and ran to them. As soon as she had touched her sister, she was stuck fast to her. So they all had to spend the night with the goose.

The next morning, Dummling took the goose under his arm and set out, without thinking much about the three girls who were stuck to it. They were obliged to run after him continually, now left, now right, wherever his legs took him.

In the middle of the fields the parson met them, and when he saw the procession he said, "For shame, you good-for-nothing girls, why are you running across the fields after this young man?" He seized the youngest girl by the hand to pull her away, but as soon as he touched her he was stuck fast too, and was obliged to run behind the rest.

Dummling, the goose, the three sisters and the parson were trotting together, one behind the other, when two labourers carrying hoes came from the fields. The parson called out to them and begged that they would set him free. But they had scarcely touched him when they were held fast, and now there were seven of them stuck to the goose, trotting along in a long line.

They came to a city, where a King ruled who had a daughter who was so serious that no one could make her laugh. The King had decreed that anyone who could make her laugh would be able to marry her. When Dummling heard this, he went before the King's daughter with his goose and the long procession and as soon as the princess saw the seven stuck people running, one behind the other, she began to laugh loudly, as if she would never stop. Dummling finally put the goose down, and all the stuck people tumbled off in a great pile, and the King's daughter laughed still more.

Dummling asked to marry her, but the King did not like the simple look of him, and to put him off said he must first produce a man who could drink a cellar of wine.

Dummling thought the little grey man might help him, so he went into the forest, and in the same place where he had felled the tree, he saw a man, who had a very sorrowful face. Dummling asked him what was wrong, and he answered, "I have such a great thirst and cannot quench it. I cannot stand water, I have just emptied a barrel of wine, but that to me is like a mere drop on a hot stone!"

"I can help you," said Dummling. "Come with me and your thirst will be quenched."

He led the man into the King's cellar. The man bent over the huge barrels, and drank and drank till his loins hurt, and before the day was out he had emptied all the barrels.

Dummling asked once more to marry the princess, but the King didn't want such an ugly fellow, whom everyone called Dummling, to take away his daughter. He made a new condition, saying Dummling must first find a man who could eat a whole mountain of bread.

Dummling found a man in the forest who said, "I have eaten a whole oven-ful of rolls, but I am still hungry. Whatever shall I do?"

Dummling led the man to the King's palace, where all the flour in the whole kingdom was collected, and from it a huge mountain of bread was baked. The man from the forest began to eat, and by the end of one day the whole mountain had vanished.

Then Dummling for the third time asked for his bride, but the King again sought a way out, and ordered he find a ship that could sail on land and on water. "As soon as you come sailing back in it," said he, "you shall have my daughter for a wife."

Dummling went straight into the forest, and the little grey man said, "I will give you the ship, because you once were kind to me."

Then he gave him a ship that could sail on land and water, and when the King saw it, he could no longer prevent Dummling from marrying his daughter. The wedding was celebrated and, after the King's death, Dummling inherited his kingdom and lived for a long time contentedly with his wife.

19

Jorinda and Jorindel

There was once a castle that stood in a deep gloomy wood, and in the castle lived an old fairy. This fairy could take any shape she pleased. All day long she flew about in the form of an owl, or crept about like a cat, but at night she became an old woman again. When any young man came within a hundred paces of her castle, he became fixed like a statue, and could not move a step till she came and set him free, which she would only do when he had given her his word never to come near again. When any young girl approached, she was changed into a bird and the fairy would put her into a cage and hang her up in the castle. There were seven hundred of these cages hanging in the castle, all with beautiful birds in them.

Now there was a girl whose name was Jorinda. She was prettier than all the pretty girls that ever were seen before. A shepherd lad, whose name was Jorindel, was very fond of her, and they were soon to be married. One day they went walking in the wood, so they could be alone. Jorindel said, "We must take care not to go too near the fairy's castle."

It was a beautiful evening; the last rays of the setting sun shone bright through the long stems of the trees upon the green undergrowth beneath, and the turtledoves sang from the tall birches.

Jorinda sat down to gaze upon the sun. Jorindel sat by her side, and both felt sad, though they didn't know why, but it was as if they were about to be parted from one another forever.

They had wandered a long way, and weren't sure which path to take home. The sun was setting fast; already half of its circle had sunk behind the hill. Jorindel looked behind him, and saw through the bushes that they had, without knowing it, sat down close to the old walls of the castle. Then he shrank with fear, turned pale, and trembled.

Jorinda was singing, but her song abruptly ended with a strange, mournful noise. Jorindel turned to see why and saw that his Jorinda was changed into a nightingale.

An owl with fiery eyes flew three times round them, and three times screamed, "To woo! To woo! To woo!"

Jorindel could not move; he stood fixed as a stone, and could neither weep, nor speak, nor stir hand or foot.

Night came. The owl flew into a bush, and a moment later the old fairy stepped out, pale and thin, with staring eyes, and a nose and chin that almost met one another.

She seized the nightingale, and went away with it in her hand. Poor Jorindel could not speak, he could not move from the spot where he stood.

At last the fairy returned and sang with a hoarse voice,

Till the prisoner is fast,
And her doom is cast,
There stay! Oh, stay!

When the charm is around her,
And the spell has bound her,
Run away! Away!

Then Jorindel found himself free. He fell on his knees before the fairy, and begged her to give him back his dear Jorinda, but she laughed at him, and said he would never see his love again. Then she went on her way.

Jorindel prayed, he wept, he sorrowed, but all in vain. "Alas!" he said, "what will become of me?" He could not bear to go back home, so he took work as a shepherd in a strange village nearer the castle. Many times he walked round and round as close to the hated walls as he dared go, but he heard and saw nothing of Jorinda.

At last he dreamt one night that he found a beautiful purple flower, and that in the middle of it lay a precious pearl, and he dreamt that he plucked the flower, and went with it in his hand into the castle, and that everything he touched with it was disenchanted, and that there he found his Jorinda again.

In the morning when he awoke, he began to search over hill and dale for this pretty flower. Eight long days he sought for it in vain, but on the ninth day, early in the morning, he found the beautiful purple flower; and in the middle of it was a dewdrop, as big as a precious pearl. He plucked the flower, and travelled day and night till he came again to the castle.

Jorindel walked closer, and did not become fixed as before, but found that he could approach the doors. He was very glad indeed of this. When he touched the door with the flower, it sprang open. He went in through the court, and heard many birds singing. At last he came to the chamber where the fairy sat, with seven hundred birds singing in the seven hundred cages. When the fairy saw Jorindel she was very angry, and screamed with rage, but she could not come within two yards of him, because the flower in his hand protected him.

He looked around at the birds, but – alas! – there were many, many nightingales. How could he know which was his Jorinda? While he was wondering what to do, he saw that the fairy had taken down one of the cages, and was heading out through the door. He ran after her, touched the cage with the flower, and Jorinda stood before him. She threw her arms round his neck, looking as beautiful as ever – as beautiful as when they walked together in the wood.

Then he touched all the other birds with the flower, and they turned back into girls again and were free. He took Jorinda home, where they were married, and lived happily together for many long years.

20

The Goose Girl

Once upon a time there was an old Queen who had a beautiful daughter. When the princess grew up she was engaged to marry a prince who lived a long way away. The time came for her to be married, and she prepared to travel to the distant kingdom. The aged Queen packed up many precious jars of silver and gold, and trinkets of gold and silver, for she loved her daughter with all her heart. She also sent her waiting maid to ride with the princess, assist her, and hand her to the bridegroom. The princess and the waiting maid each had a horse for the journey, but the horse of the Queen's daughter was called Falada, and could speak.

When the hour of parting came, the aged Queen went to her bedroom, took a small knife and cut her finger with it so it bled. Then she held a white handkerchief below, into which she let three drops of blood fall, gave it to her daughter and said, "Dear child, keep this carefully, it will help you on your way."

They said sorrowful farewells. The princess tucked the handkerchief near her heart, mounted her horse, and then went away to her bridegroom.

After she had ridden for a while she felt a burning thirst, and said to the waiting maid, "I'd like to drink. Take the golden cup you have brought for me, and please get me some water from the stream."

"If you are thirsty," said the waiting maid, "get off your horse yourself, lie down and drink out of the stream. I don't choose to be your servant."

So in her great thirst the princess alighted, bent down over the water and drank. Then she said, "Ah, Heaven!"

The three drops of blood answered, "If this your mother knew, her heart would break in two."

But the Queen's daughter was humble, said nothing, and mounted her horse again.

She rode some miles further, but the day was warm, the sun scorched her, and she was thirsty once more. When they came to another stream, she again asked her waiting maid to fill her golden cup. But the maid said still more haughtily, "If you wish to drink, get it yourself. I don't choose to be your maid."

In her great thirst the princess alighted, bent over the flowing stream, wept and said, "Ah, Heaven!"

The drops of blood again replied, "If this your mother knew, her heart would break in two." But as the Queen's daughter was drinking and leaning over the stream, the handkerchief with the three drops of blood fell down and floated away without her seeing it.

The waiting maid, however, had seen it, and she rejoiced, thinking that she now had the upper hand, for since the princess had lost the drops of the Queen's blood, she had become weak and powerless. When the princess went to mount her horse, Falada, again, the waiting maid said, "Falada is more suitable for me, and my nag will do for you."

Then the waiting maid, with threats and hard words, made the princess exchange her royal clothes for her own shabby garments, and compelled her to swear by the clear sky above her that she would not say one word of this to anyone at the royal court. If the princess had not taken this oath, she would have been killed on the spot.

But Falada saw all this.

The waiting maid now mounted Falada, and the true bride mounted the bad horse, and they travelled onwards, until at length they entered the royal palace. There were great rejoicings at their arrival. The prince sprang forward to meet the princess, but lifted the waiting maid from her horse, thinking she was his bride. She was taken upstairs, and the real princess was left standing below.

The old King looked out of the window and saw the girl in humble clothing standing in the courtyard. He noticed how dainty and delicate and beautiful she was, and went to the royal apartment to ask his son's bride who the girl she had with her was, the one standing down below in the courtyard.

The false bride said, "I picked her up on my way to be a companion. Give her something to work at, so she does not stand idle."

The old King said, "I have a little boy who tends the geese; she may help him." The goose boy was called Conrad, and the true princess became a goose girl.

Soon afterwards, the false bride said to the prince, "Dearest husband, I beg you, take the horse on which I rode here and tell the knacker to cut off his head, for he was troublesome on the way." She was afraid that the talking horse might tell what it had seen and heard.

The prince promised.

The real princess heard that the faithful Falada was to die, and she secretly arranged to pay the knacker a piece of gold if he would do something for her. There was a great dark gateway in the town, through which she passed with the geese every morning and evening. She asked the knacker to nail Falada's head over the gateway, so that she might see him again.

Early in the morning, when the princess and Conrad drove their flock beneath the dark gateway, she said in passing, "Alas, Falada, hanging there!"

Then the head answered,

> Alas, princess, how ill you fare!
> If this your mother knew,
> Her heart would break in two.

The princess and the goose boy drove their geese into the country. When they reached a meadow, she sat down and unbound her pure gold hair. Conrad saw it and delighted in its brightness, and wanted to pluck out a few strands. She said,

> Blow, blow, you gentle wind, I say,
> Blow Conrad's little hat away.
> Make him chase it here and there,
> Till I have braided all my hair,
> And bound it up again.

And there came such a violent wind that it blew Conrad's hat far across the meadows, and he was forced to run after it. When he came back she had finished combing her hair and was putting it up again, and he could not get any of it. Then Conrad was angry, and would not speak to her while they watched the geese.

Next day when they were driving the geese out through the dark gateway, the princess said, "Alas, Falada, hanging there!"

Falada answered,

Alas, princess, how ill you fare!
If this your mother knew,
Her heart would break in two.

When she again began to comb her hair in the meadow,
Conrad tried to clutch it, so she said in haste,

Blow, blow, you gentle wind, I say,
Blow Conrad's little hat away.
Make him chase it here and there,
Till I have braided all my hair,
And bound it up again.

The wind blew Conrad's hat off his head and he was
forced to run after it, and when he came back, her hair was
put up, and he could get none of it.

In the evening after they had got home, Conrad went to the old King and said, "I won't tend the geese with that girl any longer!"

The aged King asked the boy to tell him what the girl did that vexed him. Conrad said, "In the morning when we pass beneath the dark gateway with the flock, there is a horse's head on the wall, and she says to it, 'Alas, Falada, hanging there!' And the head replies,

> Alas, princess how ill you fare!
> If this your mother knew,
> Her heart would break in two."

And Conrad told the old King how the girl commanded the wind so he could not steal her golden hair.

The King told him to drive his flock out again the next day.

When morning came, the old ruler placed himself behind the dark gateway and heard how the princess spoke to the head of Falada. Then he went into the country, and hid himself in a thicket in the meadow. There he soon saw with his own eyes how radiant the girl's hair was and how she commanded the wind. Then, quite unseen, he went away.

When the goose girl came home in the evening, he called her aside, and asked why she did all these things.

"I may not tell that. I dare not lament my sorrows to any human being, for I have sworn not to do so by the Heaven above me. If I had not sworn, I would have lost my life."

He urged her, but could draw nothing from her. Then he said, "If you will not tell me anything, tell your sorrows to the iron stove there," and he went away.

Then she crept to the iron stove, and began to weep and lament, and emptied her whole heart. She said, "Here am I deserted by the whole world, and yet I am a Queen's daughter. A false waiting maid has laid me low. She compelled me to give her my royal clothes. She has taken my place with my bridegroom, and I must be a goose girl. If this my mother knew, her heart would break in two."

The aged King, however, was standing outside by the pipe of the stove, and was listening to what she said. He returned to the room, and asked her to come to him. Royal garments were placed on her, and it was marvellous how beautiful she was! The aged King summoned his son, and revealed to him that he had got the false bride, but that the true princess was standing there, the former goose girl.

The prince rejoiced with all his heart when he saw the princess's beauty and youth, and a great feast was made ready to which all the people were invited. At the head of the table sat the prince with the princess on one side of him, and the false bride on the other, but the false bride did not recognise the princess in her dazzling dress.

When they had eaten and drunk, the aged King asked the false bride a riddle about what punishment a person deserved who had behaved in such and such a way, and related the whole story.

Then the false bride said, "Such a person deserves no better fate than to be stripped entirely naked and put in a barrel that is studded inside with pointed nails. Two white horses should be harnessed to it, which will drag her along through one street after another, till she is dead."

"It is you," said the aged King. "You have pronounced your own sentence, and this is what will be done to you." When the sentence had been carried out, the prince married his true bride, and both of them reigned over their kingdom in peace and happiness.

21

The Two Kings' Children

Once upon a time there was a young son of a King who went hunting when he was sixteen years of age. In the forest he was separated from the other huntsmen. He saw a great stag that he wanted to shoot, but could not hit. He chased the stag right out of the forest, when suddenly a great tall man was standing there instead of the stag. The tall man dragged the King's son with him, taking him across a great lake to a great palace. There, they sat down at a table to eat together.

When they had eaten, the great tall man said, "I am a King, and I have a daughter. You must keep watch over her for one night, from nine in the evening till six in the morning. Every time the clock strikes, I will come and call, and if ever you give me no answer, tomorrow morning you will be put to death; but if you always give me an answer, you and she will marry."

When the young pair went to the bedroom, a stone image of Saint Christopher stood in it, and the tall King's daughter said to it, "My father will come at nine o'clock, and every hour thereafter. Every time he calls, you will answer him instead of the King's son." The stone image of Saint Christopher nodded its head quite quickly, and then more and more slowly, till at last it stood still. The King's son lay down on the threshold, put his hand under his head and slept.

The next morning the tall King said to the King's son, "You have done well, but I cannot give my daughter away yet. I have a great forest; if you cut it down for me between six o'clock this morning and six at night, I will think about it." He gave the boy a glass axe, a glass wedge and a glass mallet. When the King's son got into the forest, he began at once to chop trees, but the axe broke in two. Then he took the wedge, and struck it once with the mallet, but it became as short and as small as sand. Then he was very worried, and sat down and wept.

At noon the tall King's daughter took the boy something to eat. She asked him how he was getting on.

"Oh," he said, "I am getting on very badly."

Then she said he should come and just eat a little.

"No," said he, "I cannot do that; I will die soon, so I will eat no more."

But she spoke so kindly to him that he came and ate something. Then she said, "I will comb your hair a while, and then you will feel happier."

So she combed his hair, and he became weary and fell asleep. She took her handkerchief, made a knot in it, and struck it three times on the earth, saying, "Earth workers, come forth!"

Many little men of the earth emerged, and asked what the King's daughter commanded.

Then she said, "In three hours' time the great forest must be cut down, and the whole of the wood laid in heaps."

So the little men of the earth got together the whole of their large families to help them with the work. They began at once, and when the three hours were over, it was all done.

When the King's son awoke, he was delighted, and the tall King's daughter said, "Come home when it has struck six o'clock."

He did as she told him, and the tall King asked, "Have you cut down the forest?"

"Yes," said the King's son.

But the tall King said, "I cannot yet let you marry my daughter; you must still do something more for her sake. I have a great fish pond. You must go to it tomorrow morning and clear it of all mud until it is as bright as a mirror, and fill it with every kind of fish before six o'clock." And the tall King gave him a glass shovel and a glass hoe.

The King's son went away, and when he came to the fishpond he stuck his shovel in the mud and it broke in two, then he stuck his hoe in the mud, and broke it as well. Then he was very worried.

At noon the tall King's daughter brought him something to eat, and asked him how he was getting on.

The King's son said everything was going very badly for him, and he would certainly lose his head in the morning. "My tools have broken to pieces again."

"Oh," said she, "you must just come and eat something, and then you will be in another frame of mind." At last he came and had some bread. Then she combed his hair again, and he fell asleep, so once more she took her handkerchief, tied a knot in it, and struck the ground three times with the knot, saying, "Earth workers, come forth!"

In a moment, a great many little men of the earth came and asked what she desired, and she told them that in three

153

hours time, they must have the fish pond entirely cleaned: so clear that people could see themselves reflected in it, and every kind of fish must be in it. The little men of the earth summoned all their family and friends to help them, and in two hours it was done.

When the King's son woke, the fish pond was clear and full. He told the tall King, who said once more, "You have certainly cleared the fish pond, but I cannot give you my daughter yet; you must just do one thing more."

"What is that, then?" asked the King's son.

The tall King said he had a great mountain on which there was nothing but briars that must all be cut down, and at the top of it the boy must build a great castle, which must be stronger than he could imagine, and full of beautiful furniture.

When the King's son arose next morning, the tall King gave him a glass axe and a glass drill, and told him to have it all done by six o'clock.

As the boy was cutting down the first briar with the axe, it broke off short, and the drill also broke. Then he was quite miserable, and waited for his dearest to see if she would come and help him.

At midday, she came and brought him something to eat.

He went to meet her and told her everything, and ate something, and let her comb his hair, and he fell asleep. Then she once more took the knot and struck the earth with it, and said, "Earth workers, come forth!" Then once again a great many men of the earth came and asked what she desired. She said that in the space of three hours they must cut down all the briars and build a strong castle on top of the mountain, and fill it with beautiful furniture. The men of the earth went away and summoned their family and friends and acquaintances to help them, so when the time came, all was ready.

When the King's son woke and saw everything done, he was as happy as a bird in air.

But the tall King still said, "I cannot give away my daughter yet."

Then the King's son and the tall King's daughter felt troubled, and had no idea what to do. They ran away together that night.

When they had got a little distance away, the tall King's daughter peeped round and saw her father following them. She said, "Oh! My father is behind us, and will take us back with him. I will change you into a briar, and myself into a rose, and I will shelter myself in the middle of all your branches."

When her father reached them, there stood a briar with one rose on it. He reached to pick the rose but a thorn pricked his finger. Frustrated, he went home again. His wife asked why he hadn't brought their daughter back. He said he had nearly caught up with her, but that all at once he had lost sight of her, and a briar with one rose was growing on the spot.

Then the Queen said wisely, "If you had picked the rose, the briar would have been forced to come too."

So he went back again, but the two were already far over the plain, so the tall King ran on after them. His daughter once more looked round and saw her father coming, and said, "Oh, what shall we do now? I will instantly change you into a church and myself into a priest, and I will stand up in the pulpit and preach." When the King got to the place, there stood a church, and in the pulpit was a priest preaching. So he listened to the sermon, and then went home again.

The Queen asked why he had not brought their daughter with him, and he said, "I ran after her for a long time, and just as I thought I would soon overtake her, a church was standing there and a priest was in the pulpit preaching."

"You should just have brought the priest," said his wife wisely, "and then the church would have come too. It is no use to send you; I must go myself."

The tall King's daughter peeped round and saw the Queen coming, and said, "Now we are in trouble, for my mother is coming herself: I will immediately change you into a fish pond and myself into a fish."

When her mother came to the place, there was a large fish pond, and in the middle of it a fish was leaping about and peeping out of the water quite merrily. The mother wanted to catch the fish, but she could not. Then she was very angry, and drank up the whole pond in order to catch the fish, but it made her so ill that she was forced to vomit it all out again. Then she said, "I see very well that nothing can be done now. You might as well stop your disguising."

They did, and the Queen gave her daughter three walnuts, saying, "These will help you when you are in greatest need."

The young folk travelled on together. After many days, they arrived at the castle the King's son had come from, and close by it was a village. The King's son said, "Stay here in

the village, my dearest. I will just go to the castle, and then I will come with a carriage and attendants to fetch you."

When he got to the castle, all there rejoiced greatly at having him back home, and he told them he had a bride who was now in the village. They harnessed the horses at once, and many attendants seated themselves upon the carriage. Then, just when the King's son was about to get in, his mother gave him a kiss, and he forgot everything that had happened, and also what he was about to do.

His mother ordered the horses to be unharnessed from the carriage again, and everyone went back into the castle. The tall King's daughter sat in the village and watched and watched, and thought the King's son would come and fetch her, but no one came. So she started to work in the mill that belonged to the castle.

A long time passed, during which the girl worked for the miller honourably and faithfully. In the meantime, the Queen had found a wife for her son from a distant part of the world. They were to be married as soon as the bride arrived. Many people gathered to see the wedding. The tall King's daughter asked the miller if she could go too, and the miller said yes.

When she was about to go, the tall King's daughter opened one of the three walnuts her mother had given her, and a beautiful dress lay inside it. She put it on, and went into the church and stood by the altar. The bride and bridegroom came in and seated themselves in front of the altar. When the priest was going to bless them, the bride peeped half round and saw the girl standing there. Then the bride stood up, and said she would not be married until she had a dress as beautiful as the one worn by that lady there.

They asked the girl from the mill whether she would sell her dress. No, she would not sell it, but she said the bride might perhaps earn it. The bride asked how. The tall King's daughter said that she wanted to sleep one night outside the King's son's door. If she could do that, the bride could have what she wanted.

The bride arranged this, and the tall King's daughter laid herself down outside the King's son's door and lamented all night long. She had the forest cut down for him, she had the fish pond cleaned out for him, she had the castle built for him, she had changed him into a briar, and then into a church, and at last into a fish pond, and yet he had forgotten her so quickly. The Kings son's servant had been ordered to give him a sleeping potion. He slept so heavily, he did not hear one word of the lament.

But the servant heard it and wondered what it meant.

The next morning, the bride put on the beautiful dress and went away to the church with the bridegroom.

The tall King's daughter opened the second walnut, and a still more beautiful dress was inside it. She put it on, and went and stood by the altar in the church, and everything happened as it had happened before.

The tall King's daughter again lay all night outside the door of the King's son's chamber, and the servant was once more supposed to give him a sleeping potion. But instead, the servant gave him something that would keep him awake. This time the King's son heard the girl outside his door, and was very troubled; what was past came back to him.

The next morning, he went at once to his beloved, the tall King's daughter, and explained everything that had happened to him, and begged her not to be angry with him for having forgotten her.

The tall King's daughter opened the third walnut, and within it was a still more magnificent dress, which she put on, and she went with her bridegroom to church. Children came and gave them flowers and ribbons to bind around their feet, and they were blessed by the priest, and had a happy wedding.

His mother and the bride from a distant land had to leave.

And the mouth of the person who last told all this is still warm.

22

The Clever Little Tailor

Once upon a time there was a princess who was extremely proud. If a young man came to see her she would give him a riddle to guess, and if he could not figure out the answer, she would send him contemptuously away. She told everyone that she would marry the man who was able to solve her riddle, no matter who he was.

Three tailors decided they would try together. The two eldest thought they had done so many dexterous, difficult sewing tasks successfully that they were bound to succeed at the riddle as well. The third, youngest tailor was down at heel and was no good at his work, but thought he must have some luck with the riddle, for where else was success to come from? The two others said to him, "Just stay at home; you can't do much with a brain like yours." But the little tailor refused to be discouraged, and said he would manage well enough. He went forth as if the whole world were his.

They went to the princess, and said she should ask her riddle, and that their thinking was so fine it could be threaded through a needle. The princess said, "I have two kinds of hair on my head, what colours are they?"

The first tailor answered, "It must be black and white, like the cloth called 'pepper and salt'."

The princess said, "Wrong guess; let the second man answer."

The second tailor said, "If it's not black and white, then it is brown and red, like my father's company coat."

"Wrong guess," said the princess, "let the third man give an answer."

Then the little tailor stepped boldly forth and said, "The princess has silver and golden hair on her head: those are the two different colours."

When the princess heard this answer, she turned pale and nearly fell down with terror, for the little tailor had guessed her riddle, and she had firmly believed that no man on earth could solve it. When her courage returned she said, "You cannot marry me yet; there is something more you must do. Below, in the stable is a bear. You must pass the night with it. When I get up in the morning, if you are still alive, you shall marry me." She expected that this would get rid of the little tailor, for no one had ever survived falling into the clutches of the bear.

The little tailor refused to be frightened. He was quite delighted, and said, "Boldly ventured is half won."

When evening came, the little tailor was taken down to the bear. The bear growled and was about to hit the little fellow with his paws, but, "Softly, softly," said the little tailor, "I will soon make you quiet." Then quite composedly, as if he had not an anxiety in the world, he took some nuts out of his pocket, cracked them, and ate the kernels. When the bear saw this, he was seized with a desire for nuts. The tailor reached into his pockets for a handful, but these were pebbles instead of nuts.

The bear put them in his mouth, but could get nothing out of them, no matter how hard he bit. *What a stupid blockhead I am!* thought he, *I cannot even crack a nut!* Then he said to the tailor, "Here, crack me the nuts."

"There, see what a stupid fellow you are!" said the little tailor. "Fancy having such a great mouth, and not being able to crack a small nut!" Then he took the pebble but nimbly put a nut in his mouth instead, and crack, it was broken in two!

"I must try the thing again," said the bear. "When I watch you, I feel I ought to be able to do it also." So the tailor once more gave him a pebble, and the bear tried and tried to bite into it with all the strength of his body. But of course he could not.

Then the tailor took out a violin from beneath his coat, and played to himself. When the bear heard the music, he could not help dancing, and when he had danced a while, he was so happy that he said to the little tailor, "Tell me, is the fiddle heavy?"

"Light enough for a child. Look, with the left hand I lay my fingers on it, and with the right I stroke it with the bow, and then it sings merrily, tum-ta-tum-ta-tum!"

"Well," said the bear, "I would like to learn to play the violin, so I could dance whenever I wanted. Will you give me lessons?"

"With all my heart," said the tailor, "if you have a talent for it. But just let me see your claws... They are terribly long; I must cut your nails a little." Then a vice was brought, and the bear put his claws in it, and the little tailor screwed it tight, and said, "Now wait until I come with the scissors." Then he let the bear growl as much as he liked, lay down in the corner on a bundle of straw, and fell asleep.

When the princess heard the bear growling so fiercely during the night, she suspected only that he was growling for joy, and had killed the tailor. In the morning she rose carefree and happy, but when she peeped into the bear's stable, the tailor stood cheerfully before her, as healthy as a fish in water. Now she could not say another word against the wedding because she had given a promise in front of everyone.

The little tailor and the princess got into her carriage, setting off to the church to be married. But then the two older tailors, who had false hearts, and were jealous of the little tailor who had succeeded where they had failed, went into the stable and unscrewed the bear again. The bear ran after the carriage in great fury. The princess heard him snorting and growling. She was terrified, and cried, "The bear is behind us and wants to get you!"

The tailor was quick. He stood on his head, stuck his legs out the window, and cried, "Do you see the vice? Be off, or you will be locked into it again." The bear turned round and ran away.

The clever little tailor drove quietly to church, and the princess was married to him, and he lived with her as happy as a woodlark.

And whoever does not believe this must pay a silver coin.

23

The Four Skilful Brothers

There was once a poor man who had four sons. When they had grown up, he said to them, "My dear children, you must now go out into the world, for I have nothing to give you. Go abroad and learn a trade, and see whether you can make a living." So the four brothers took their sticks, said farewell to their father, and travelled off together.

After some time, they came to a crossroads that branched in four different directions. The eldest said, "Here we must separate, but on this day in four years' time we will meet again at this spot. In the meantime we will seek our fortunes." Then each of them went his way.

The eldest met a man who asked him where he was going, and what he was intending to do. "I want to learn a trade," he replied.

Then the man said, "Come with me and be a thief."

"No," the eldest answered, "that is not a reputable trade, and it ends with swinging on the gallows."

"Oh," said the man, "you need not be afraid of the gallows. I will teach you to steal things no one else could, and no one will ever detect you."

The eldest brother was talked into it, and became an accomplished thief. He was so dexterous that nothing he desired was safe from him.

The second brother met a man who asked him what he wanted to learn in the world.

"I don't know yet," the second brother replied.

"Then come with me, and be an astronomer; there is no better profession, for nothing is hidden from one who can see the stars."

The second brother liked the idea, and became such a skilful astronomer that his master gave him a telescope and said, "With this you can see everything on earth or in heaven; nothing can be concealed from you."

A huntsman took the third brother into training, and gave him excellent instruction. Once he was experienced, the huntsman gave him a gun and said, "It will never fail you; you are certain to hit whatever you aim at."

The fourth, youngest brother also met a man who inquired what his intentions were. "Wouldn't you like to be a tailor?" the man asked.

"No, I don't think so," said the youth. "Sitting doubled up from morning till night driving the needle backwards and forwards doesn't appeal to me."

"Oh, but you are speaking in ignorance," answered the man. "With me you would learn a very different kind of tailoring, one that is useful, honourable and full of interest." The youngest brother let himself be persuaded, and went with the man to learn his art. When they eventually parted, the man gave the youth a needle, and said, "With this you can sew together whatever you are given, whether it is as soft as an egg or as hard as steel, and it will all become one piece, so that no seam will be visible."

When the four years were over, the four brothers arrived back at the crossroads, embraced each other, and returned home to their father. "So now," said he, quite delighted, "the wind has blown you back again to me." They told him that each had learnt his own trade.

They were sitting in front of their house under a large tree, and the father said, "I will put you all to the test, to see what you can do." He looked up and said to his second son, "Between two branches at the top of this tree, there is a chaffinch's nest. Tell me how many eggs there are in it."

The astronomer took his telescope, looked up and said, "There are five."

Then the father said to the eldest brother, "Fetch the eggs down without disturbing the bird sitting on them." The skilful thief climbed up, and took the five eggs from beneath the bird. She never noticed what he was doing, and remained quietly sitting where she was. He brought them down to his father.

The father took them, placed them in a row down the table, and said to the huntsman, "With one shot, shoot the five eggs in two, through the middle." The huntsman aimed, and with one shot broke all five eggs, as the father had asked.

"Now it's your turn," said the father to the fourth son. "You will sew the eggs together again, and the young birds inside them as well, and you must do it so that they are

not hurt by the shot." The tailor brought his needle, and sewed them as his father wished.

Then the thief climbed up the tree again, and put the mended eggs back under the bird without her being aware of it. After a few days, the eggs hatched and the baby birds crept out. They had a red line round their necks where they had been sewn together by the tailor.

"Well," said the old man to his sons, "you really ought to be praised to the skies. You have used your time admirably, and have each learnt something that will serve you well. I can't say which of your professions will be the most useful. That will be proved with time and opportunity."

Not long after this, there was a great uproar in the country because a dragon had carried off the King's daughter. The King was deeply troubled. He proclaimed that whoever brought the princess back would be married to her.

The four brothers said to each other, "Here is a fine opportunity to show what we can do."

"I will soon know where she is," said the astronomer, and looked through his telescope. "I see her already: she is far away from here on a rock in the sea, and the dragon is beside her watching her."

He went to the King, and asked for a ship for himself and his brothers. They sailed over the sea until they came to the rock where the King's daughter was sitting, with the dragon lying asleep on her lap. The huntsman said, "I dare not shoot the dragon, I could kill the beautiful girl at the same time."

"Then I will try my art," said the thief. He crept to the rock and stole the girl from under the dragon so quietly and dexterously that the monster never noticed it, but went on snoring.

Full of joy, they hurried off with her, steering the ship out into the open sea. But then the dragon woke and, finding no princess there, followed the ship, snorting angrily through the air. Just as he was circling, about to descend onto them, the huntsman shouldered his gun, and shot him through the heart. The monster fell down dead, but was so large and powerful that his fall shattered the whole ship.

The four brothers and the princess caught hold of planks to keep afloat, but they were in peril on the wide sea. Then the tailor took his wondrous needle and, with a few stitches, sewed the planks together. They all sat on this raft and collected the fragments of the ship. The tailor sewed these so skilfully together that in a very short time the ship was once more seaworthy, and they could go home.

When the King had his daughter back safely there was great rejoicing. He said to the four brothers, "One of you can marry her, but you must settle among yourselves which of you it is to be."

Then a heated argument arose among them, as each thought his own trade was the most vital. The astronomer said to his brothers, "If I had not seen the princess, all your arts would have been useless."

The thief said, "What would have been the use of your seeing, if I had not got her away from the dragon?"

The huntsman said, "You three and the princess would have been torn to pieces by the dragon if my shot had not hit him."

The tailor said, "And if I, by my art, had not sewn the ship together again, you would all have been miserably drowned."

The King, listening, pronounced his verdict. "Each one of you has an equal right, and as you cannot all have the princess, none of you shall have her. Instead I will give each of you a quarter of the kingdom as a reward."

The brothers were pleased with this decision, and said that was much better than fighting with each other. Each of them received a quarter of the kingdom, and they lived with their father in the greatest happiness as long as it pleased God.

24

One-Eye, Two-Eyes, Three-Eyes

There was once a woman who had three daughters. The eldest was called One-eye, because she had only one eye in the middle of her forehead; the second, Two-eyes, because she had two eyes like other people; the youngest, Three-eyes, because she had three eyes, and her third eye was also in the centre of her forehead.

As Two-eyes looked just like other people, her sisters and her mother could not stand her. They said to her, "You with your two eyes are no better than the common people: you do not belong to us!" They pushed her about, gave her nothing to eat but scraps and leftovers, and did everything they could to make her unhappy.

One day, Two-eyes had to go out into the fields and tend the goat, but she was still hungry because her sisters had given her very little to eat. She sat on a ridge and wept so bitterly that two streams ran down from her eyes. When she looked up in her grief, a woman was standing beside her, who said, "Why are you weeping, little Two-eyes?"

Two-eyes answered, "My sisters and mother hate me for my two eyes. They push me from one corner to another, and give me nothing to eat but scraps. I am so hungry."

The Wise Woman said, "Wipe away your tears, Two-eyes, and I will tell you something that will prevent you ever again suffering from hunger: just say to your goat,

> Bleat, my little goat, bleat,
> Cover the table with something to eat.

"Then a pretty little table will stand before you, with the most delicious food upon it. When you have eaten enough, just say,

> Bleat, bleat, my little goat, I pray,
> And take the table quite away.

Then the table will vanish." Having said this, the Wise Woman left.

Two-eyes thought, *I must try this right away, for I am so terribly hungry.* And she said,

> Bleat, my little goat, bleat,
> Cover the table with something to eat.

Scarcely had she spoken the words than a little table covered with a white cloth stood before her. On it was a plate, a silver spoon and the most delicious food, warm and smoking as if it had just come from the kitchen. Two-eyes said the shortest prayer she knew, "Lord God, be with us always, Amen," and helped herself to some food, and enjoyed it. When she was satisfied, she said,

Bleat, bleat, my little goat, I pray,
And take the table quite away.

Immediately the little table and everything on it were gone. *That is a delightful way of clearing up!* thought Two-eyes, and she was glad and happy.

In the evening when she went home with her goat, she found a small earthenware dish with some scraps in it her sisters had left her, but she did not touch them. The next day she left untouched the few bits of broken bread that had been handed to her. Her mother and sisters did not notice at first, but when they realised it happened every time, they said, "Two-eyes now always leaves her scraps untouched. She used to eat everything we gave her; she must have discovered another way to get food." They resolved to send One-eye with Two-eyes to the pasture, to see whether anyone brought her anything to eat.

So, when Two-eyes next set out, One-eye went with her. Two-eyes knew what One-eye must be looking for. She drove the goat into high grass and said, "Come, One-eye, we will sit down, and I will sing something to you." One-eye

was tired with the unaccustomed walk and the heat of the sun, and Two-eyes sang,

> One eye, are you waking?
> One eye, are you sleeping?

One-eye shut her one eye, and fell asleep.

Only then did Two-eyes call on her goat to give her the little table. Then, once she'd eaten, Two-eyes woke One-eye, scolding her sister, "One-eye, you go to sleep while you are caring for the goat! It could run away and be lost. Come, let us go home." They went home, and again Two-eyes left her little dish untouched, but One-eye could not tell her mother why.

Next day the mother told Three-eyes to go with her sister and see whether she ate anything or anyone brought her food. Two-eyes and Three-eyes went off with the goat, but Two-eyes knew what must be in Three-eyes' mind. She drove the goat into high grass and said, "We will sit down, and I will sing to you, Three-eyes." Three-eyes was tired with the walk and with the heat of the sun, and Two-eyes sang the same song as before,

> Three eyes, are you waking?

But then, instead of singing *Three eyes, are you sleeping?* as she ought to have done, she thoughtlessly sang,

> Two eyes, are you sleeping?

Then two of Three-eyes' eyes closed and fell asleep, but the third, which had not been named in the song, stayed awake. Three-eyes shut it, but only to pretend it was asleep too. It blinked, and could see everything very well.

When Two-eyes thought that Three-eyes was fast asleep, she said,

> Bleat, my little goat, bleat,
> Cover the table with something to eat.

She ate and drank her fill, then ordered the table to go away again,

> Bleat, bleat, my little goat, I pray,
> And take the table quite away.

Three-eyes had seen everything. Two-eyes woke her and said, "Have you been asleep, Three-eyes? What kind of a caretaker are you? Come, we will go home." When they got home, Two-eyes again did not eat and Three-eyes said to their mother, "I know why she does not eat. When she is out, she says to the goat,

> Bleat, my little goat, bleat,
> Cover the table with something to eat.

Then a little table appears before her covered with much better food than we have here. When she has eaten all she wants, she says,

> Bleat, bleat, my little goat, I pray,
> And take the table quite away.

Then it all disappears. I watched everything closely. She put two of my eyes to sleep, but luckily the one in my forehead stayed awake."

Then the envious mother cried to Two-eyes, "Do you want to eat better than we do, ungrateful girl?" She fetched a butcher's knife and thrust it into the heart of the goat, which fell down dead.

When Two-eyes saw that, she was very upset and went out to the ridge of grass at the edge of the field, and wept bitter tears. Suddenly the Wise Woman stood by her side once again, and said, "Two-eyes, why are you weeping?"

"Haven't I reason to weep?" she answered. "The goat that brought me the table of food as you showed me has been killed by my mother, and now I will be hungry again."

The Wise Woman said, "Two-eyes, ask your sisters to give you the entrails of the slaughtered goat. Bury them in the ground in front of the house, and your fortune will be made." Then she vanished.

Two-eyes went home and said to her sisters, "Dear sisters, please give me some of my goat; I don't wish for the best parts, but let me have the entrails."

The sisters laughed and said, "If that's all you want, you can have them."

So Two-eyes took the entrails and buried them quietly in the evening, in front of the house, as the Wise Woman had advised.

Next morning when they all woke, a strangely magnificent tree stood outside the door. Its leaves were silver and its fruit was gold, and in all the wide world there was nothing more beautiful or precious. They did not know how the tree could have grown during the night, but Two-eyes saw that it must have come from the goat's entrails, for it was standing on the exact spot where she had buried them.

Then the mother told One-eye to climb up and gather some of the fruit, but whenever One-eye was about to get hold of one of the golden apples, the branch escaped from her hands, so that she could not pluck a single one.

The mother told Three-eyes to climb up, but she was no more able to grasp the fruit than her eldest sister. At length the mother grew impatient and climbed up herself, but she was also unable to get hold of the precious bounty and always clutched empty air.

Then Two-eyes said she would try. Her sisters cried, "You indeed, with your two eyes, what can you do?" But Two-eyes climbed up, and the golden apples came into her hand of their own accord, so that she could pluck them one after the other, and she filled her apron with precious fruit. When she climbed down, her mother took them away from her. She and One-eye and Three-eyes were jealous that she could

harvest from the tree, and they treated her still more cruelly.

Not long after came a day when they were all standing together by the tree and a young knight rode up. "Quick, Two-eyes," cried the two other sisters, "creep under this, and don't disgrace us!" They quickly turned an empty barrel over their sister.

The handsome knight stopped to admire the magnificent gold-and-silver tree, and said to the two sisters, "To whom does this wonderful tree belong? Anyone who will give me one branch of it may in return ask for anything she desires."

Then One-eye and Three-eyes replied that the tree belonged to them, and that they would give him a branch. But they were not able to grant the knight what he asked, because the branches always swayed out of their grasp.

The knight asked them whether the tree was really theirs and they assured him it was. But while they were saying so, Two-eyes rolled golden apples from under the barrel to the feet of the knight. When the knight saw the apples he was astonished, and asked where they came from. One-eye and Three-eyes answered that they had another sister, who was not allowed to show herself, for she only had two eyes like any common person. The knight, however, desired to see this other sister, and cried, "Two-eyes, come forth!"

Then Two-eyes came out from beneath the barrel, and the knight was surprised at her great beauty. He said, "I'm sure you, Two-eyes, can break a branch from the tree for me."

"Yes," replied Two-eyes, "I can, for the tree belongs to me." She climbed up, and broke off a branch with the greatest ease and gave it to the knight.

Then he said, "Two-eyes, what shall I give you for it?"

"Alas!" answered Two-eyes, "I suffer from hunger and thirst and grief, from early morning till late at night. If you will take me with you, away from these things, I will be happy." So the knight lifted Two-eyes onto his horse and took her home to his father's castle. There he gave her beautiful clothes, and meat and drink to her heart's content, and as he loved her so much, he married her, and there was great rejoicing.

When Two-eyes looked out the window of her own little room in the castle, to her great delight she saw the gold-and-silver tree, for it had followed her. She lived a long time in happiness.

One day two poor women came to her in her castle, and begged for charity. She looked closely at their faces, and recognised her sisters, One-eye and Three-eyes, who had fallen into such poverty that they had to beg for bread. Two-eyes made them welcome and took care of them, so that they both repented the evil they had done their sister with all their hearts.

25

The Star Money

Once upon a time there was a little girl whose father and mother were dead, and she was so poor that she no longer had anywhere to live or a bed to sleep in – nothing but the clothes she was wearing and a little bit of bread in her hand, which some charitable person had given to her. But she was good and honest.

As she was abandoned by all the world, she went forth into the open country, trusting in the good God to provide for her. A poor man met her, who said, "Give me something to eat, I am so hungry!" She gave him her whole piece of bread, saying, "May God bless it to your use," and went onwards. Then along came a boy who moaned, "My head is so cold, give me something to cover it." So she took off her hood and gave it to him. When she had walked a little further, she met another child who had no jacket and was frozen with cold. She gave the child her jacket. A little further on she met a child begging for a dress, so she gave her dress away also.

At length it became dark and she walked into a forest, where she met yet another child, who asked for a shirt.

The good poor girl thought to herself, "It is a dark night and no one can see me, so I can give my undershirt away." She took it off, and gave it away.

Now she didn't have a single thing left. As she stood in the darkness without anything, some stars from heaven fell down, and they turned out to be hard smooth shiny coins, and a new shirt of the very finest linen.

She gathered the coins into the front of the shirt, and was rich all the days of her life.

26

Snow White and Rose Red

There was once a poor widow who lived in a little cottage by the woods. In front of the cottage was a garden with two beautiful rose bushes. One bush bloomed with white roses and the other with red roses.

The widow had two children who were just like the roses. One was called "Snow White" and the other "Rose Red". They were as good, hard working and cheerful as any two children in the world. Snow White was quieter and more gentle than Rose Red, who loved to run about in the meadows and fields, looking for flowers and catching butterflies. Snow White would sit at home with her mother, helping with the housework or reading aloud to her when there was no work to be done.

The two children loved each other so much that they walked hand in hand whenever they left the cottage.

Snow White would say, "We will never leave each other."

Rose Red would answer, "Not as long as we live."

And their mother would add, "Whatever one has, she should share with the other."

Often they would walk in the woods, hand in hand,

gathering red berries. The animals came up to them without fear. The little hare would eat a cabbage leaf out of their hands, the roe deer grazed beside them and the hart bounded joyfully past them, while the birds stayed on their branches singing their merry songs.

No accident ever befell Snow White and Rose Red. If they stayed late in the woods and night came, they would lie side by side on a patch of moss and sleep until morning, and their mother would know they were safe.

One night in the woods, they saw a lovely child in a shining white dress sitting near where they lay. The child stood up and smiled at them, but said nothing and walked away. When they looked around they saw that they had been sleeping on a clifftop and, if they had walked a few steps further in the darkness, they would have fallen over the edge. Their mother told them that they had met the angel who watches over good children.

Snow White and Rose Red kept their mother's cottage very clean and tidy. In summer, Rose Red brought her mother a bunch of flowers every morning, with one rose from the red bush and one from the white. She put them beside her bed before she woke up. In winter Snow White lit the fire and hung the kettle on the hook. The kettle was

made of brass, but it shone like gold because it had been so well polished.

In the evenings, when the snow was falling, their mother would say, "Snow White, go and bolt the door." Then she would read aloud to them by the hearth, while the two girls sat and span. Beside them a lamb lay on the floor, and behind them on a perch sat a little white dove.

One evening, as they were sitting cosily together, someone knocked at the door. "Quick, Rose Red, go and open the door," said their mother. "It must be a traveller seeking shelter."

Rose Red drew back the bolt, thinking it would be some poor weary man, but it was not: a bear thrust his thick black head in through the doorway.

Rose Red cried out and sprang back, the lamb bleated, the little dove fluttered up into the air and Snow White hid behind her mother's bed.

But the bear spoke to them, "Do not be afraid, I will do you no harm. I am half frozen and I only wish to warm myself a little in your house."

"You poor bear," said their mother. "Lie down by the fire, but be careful not to singe your fur."

Then she called, "Snow White, Rose Red, come out. The bear will not hurt you; he can be trusted." They both came forward, and very cautiously the lamb and the dove came nearer until they were no longer afraid.

"Children," said the bear, "beat the snow a little out of my fur." They fetched a broom and swept the fur clean while he stretched out by the fire and, much at ease, growled contentedly.

Soon the girls got to know and trust their clumsy guest, and began to play mischievous games with him. They tugged at his fur with their hands, put their feet on his back and rocked him back and forth; they took a hazel branch and beat him, and when he growled they laughed. The bear did not mind at all, but when they were too rough, he cried,

Leave me alive, children,
Snow White, Rose Red,
You'll strike your suitor dead.

When it was time to go to sleep, their mother said to the bear, "In God's name you may stay and lie by the hearth and you will be sheltered from the cold and bad weather."

As soon as the grey dawn came, the two children let the bear out and he trundled off over the snow into the woods.

From then on, the bear came back every evening at the same time. He lay down by the hearth and let the children play with him as much as they wished. They were now so used to him coming that they did not bolt the door until their black companion had come in.

When spring came and the outside world was green once more, the bear said to Snow White, "Now I must go away and I cannot come back all summer."

"Where are you going, dear bear?" asked Snow White.

"I must go into the wood and guard my treasures from the wicked dwarfs. In winter when the ground is frozen hard they have to remain below and cannot work their way up and out, but now that the sun has thawed the earth, they will break through. Then they will search and steal. Whatever they take down into their holes cannot easily be brought back into the daylight."

Snow White was sad to say goodbye to her friend. When she drew back the bolt of the door and the bear pushed his way out, his fur caught on the latch and a piece of his hide was torn off. Snow White thought she saw a glimpse of gold shining through from underneath, but she couldn't be sure. The bear hurried away and soon disappeared among the trees.

After a while, their mother sent the children into the wood to gather firewood. They found a large tree that lay felled on the ground. Next to the trunk something was jumping up and down in the grass, but they couldn't make out what it was.

When they went nearer, they saw it was a dwarf with a wrinkled old face and a very long snow-white beard. The end of the beard was caught tight in a cleft of the tree, and the little man was jumping like a dog on a leash, not knowing what to do. He stared at the girls with his fiery red eyes and screamed, "What are you standing there for? Can't you come and help me?"

"What has happened to you, little man?" asked Rose Red.

"Silly nosy goose!" answered the dwarf. "I wanted to split the tree to make small logs for the kitchen fire. Thick logs burn the little food that we eat; we don't guzzle as much as you greedy folk. I had already hammered in the wedge and everything was going well, but the cursed wooden wedge flew out and the tree trunk snapped so quickly that I got my lovely white beard stuck in the tree and now I can't get away. And you silly, smooth milk-faces are laughing. Bah! How repulsive you are!"

The children tried hard, but they could not pull the beard out; it was jammed in tight.

"I'll go and get some people to help," said Rose Red.

"You mutton-headed chumps!" screeched the dwarf. "What do you want to fetch more people for? You're two too many already. Can't you think of anything better?"

"Don't be impatient," said Snow White. "I'll soon get you out." She took her scissors out of her pocket and cut off the end of his beard.

As soon as the dwarf was freed, he seized a sack of gold that was hidden behind the roots of the tree and muttered to himself, "Uncivilised rabble, cutting off a piece of my good beard – a pox on you!"

Then he slung the sack on his back, and off he went without even looking back.

Some time later, Snow White and Rose Red went to the stream to catch some fish for supper. As they came to the banks of the stream, they saw something that looked like a big grasshopper hopping towards the water's edge as if it were about to jump in. They ran up, and saw it was the dwarf.

"Where are you going?" asked Rose Red. "Surely you don't want to jump in the water?"

"I'm not a fool!" cried the dwarf. "Can't you see that the cursed fish is trying to pull me in?"

The little man had been sitting there fishing when a gust of wind had blown his beard into his fishing line and it had got tangled. When a big fish had taken a bite on his hook, the weak dwarf couldn't pull it out of the water. As the fish struggled to free itself, it pulled the dwarf after it, and although he tried to clutch at stalks and rushes to steady himself, he would soon be dragged in.

The girls had come along in the nick of time. They held the dwarf tight and tried to free his beard from the line, but beard and line were hopelessly entwined. There was nothing for it but to take out the scissors and cut away some more of the beard.

When the dwarf saw, he screamed, "Do you think that's civil, you toads, to ruin a person's face? Wasn't it enough to spoil the end of my beard, without cutting off the best part of it? I won't be able to show myself to my own people. Buzz off and run till your feet fall off!"

Then he fetched a sack of pearls, which was lying in the reeds and, without saying another word, he hauled it away and disappeared behind a stone.

Soon afterwards, their mother sent the two girls off to town to buy thread, needles, tape and ribbons. As they walked over the heath towards town, they saw a great bird hovering in the air and slowly circling above them. It sank lower and lower until it finally plunged down by one of the many rocks that lay strewn over the heath.

Immediately afterwards the girls heard a piercing cry of pain. They ran towards the sound and saw, to their horror, that the eagle had seized hold of the dwarf and was about to carry him off.

The kind children held tightly to the little man and struggled with the eagle until he let go of his prey.

When the dwarf had recovered from his fright, he cried in his screeching voice, "Couldn't you have treated me a bit more carefully? My thin coat is torn into shreds and holes, you awkward, clumsy clots!"

Then he grabbed a sack of jewels and crept under the rocks into his hole. The girls were already used to his ungrateful ways, and continued on their way to town.

When the girls came back from town over the heath towards home, they saw the dwarf once again, and took him by surprise. He was emptying his sack of jewels, for he did not think anyone would be passing by so late.

The evening sun shone on the sparkling jewels, and they glittered and gleamed so gloriously that the children stopped to look at them.

"Why are you standing and staring?" screamed the dwarf, and his ashen grey face turned scarlet with rage. He carried on shouting until they all heard a loud growling sound and a black bear came out of the wood.

The dwarf jumped up in fright, but the bear was blocking the entrance to his hidey-hole so he could not escape.

"Dear bear, spare me!" he cried out in terror. "I will give you all my treasures. See my beautiful jewels lying there? Grant me my life. I'm such a scraggy little creature, you would hardly feel me between your teeth. Look, take these two god-less girls. They would be tender morsels for you; they're as juicy as young quails. Eat them up for heaven's sake!"

The bear took no notice of his words. He gave the evil creature one single blow with his paw, and he never moved again.

The girls had run away, but the bear called after them, "Snow White and Rose Red, do not be afraid. Wait, I will come along with you."

When they heard his voice, the girls recognised their good friend, and they waited. When the bear was beside them his bearskin fell off, and there he stood: a handsome young man, dressed all in gold.

"I am the King's son," he said. "I was bewitched by the evil dwarf who stole my treasure and condemned me to roam the woods as a wild bear until I was released by his death. He has got what he deserved."

Years later, Snow White was married to the prince and

Rose Red to his brother, and they shared the great treasures that the dwarf had gathered in his hole.

Their mother lived for many years peacefully and happily with her children in the princes' palace. She took her two rose bushes with her, and they grew in front of her palace window. Every year they bore the loveliest roses, white and red.

27

Strong Hans

A man and a woman and their one child lived quite alone in a remote valley. One day the mother went into the forest to gather fir tree branches, and took little Hans, who was just two years old. It was spring, the child was enjoying the flowers, and they wandered further on. Suddenly two robbers sprang out of a thicket, seized the mother and child, and carried them far away into the black forest, where no one ever went. The poor woman begged the robbers to set them free, but their hearts were made of stone; they would not listen to her prayers and pleading, and forced her to keep walking.

After they had worked their way through bushes and briars, they came to a rock with a door in it. The robbers knocked and it opened at once. They went through a long dark passage to an underground cave. On the wall hung swords, sabers and other deadly weapons gleaming in the light, and in the middle stood a black table at which four other robbers were sitting gambling, and the captain, who sat at the head of it. He came and spoke to the woman, telling her not to fear, they wouldn't hurt her, but she must look after the housekeeping, and if she kept everything in order, she would not suffer. They gave her something to eat, and showed her a bed where she and Hans could sleep.

The woman stayed many years with the robbers, and Hans grew tall and strong. His mother told him stories, and taught him to read an old book of tales about knights that she found in the cave.

When Hans was nine years old, he made himself a strong club out of a branch of fir and hid it behind the bed. He went to his mother and said, "Dear Mother, please tell me who my father is. I must and will know." His mother would not tell him, because she didn't want him to long for their former home. She knew that the godless robbers would not let him leave, and it almost broke her heart that Hans could not know his father.

In the night, when the robbers came home from their robbing expedition, Hans brought out his club, stood before the captain, and said, "I now wish to know who my father is, and if you do not tell me, I will strike you down." The captain laughed, and gave Hans such a blow on the ear that he rolled under the table. Hans got up again, held his tongue, and thought, *I will wait another year and then try again.*

When the year was over, he brought out his club once more, rubbed the dust off it, and said, "It is a stout strong club." At night, the robbers came home and sat about drinking one jug of wine after another, and their heads began to be heavy. Then Hans brought out his club, stood before the captain, and asked once more who his father was. The captain again gave him such a vigorous blow on the ear that Hans rolled under the table. But this time he jumped up again, and beat the captain and the robbers with his club until they could no longer move their arms or legs. His mother stood in a corner

full of admiration for his bravery and strength. When Hans was finished with the robbers, he said to his mother, "Now I have shown that I am serious. I must know who my father is."

"Dear Hans," answered his mother, "come, we will seek until we find him."

She took the key to the door from the captain, and Hans packed a sack with gold and silver. They left the cave for the first time since Hans was just two years old. How his eyes opened when he came out of the darkness into daylight, and saw the green forest, and the flowers, and the birds, and the morning sun in the sky. He stood there and wondered at everything.

His mother found the right way home, and when they had walked for a long while, they got safely into their lonely valley and to their little house. Hans's father was sitting in the doorway. He wept for joy when he recognised his wife and realised Hans was his boy, because he had thought they were dead. Hans, though young, was a head taller than his father.

They went inside together, but when Hans put his sack of gold and silver on the bench by the stove, the whole house began to crack. The bench broke, and then the floor, and the heavy sack fell through into the cellar. "God save us," cried the father. "Our little house is broken to pieces."

"Don't be worried, dear Father," answered Hans. "That sack holds far more than what we'd need for a new house." Hans and his father began to build a new house, to buy cattle and land, and to keep a farm. Hans ploughed the fields, and he was so strong that when he pushed the plough, the bullocks had scarcely any need to pull.

The next spring, Hans said to his parents, "Keep all the gold and silver, but order me a walking stick that weighs a hundred tons, and I will go travelling." When the stick was ready, he left his parents and went forth into the world.

When he came to a deep dark forest, he heard something crunching and cracking. Looking about, he saw a fir tree that was wound round like a rope from the bottom to the top. A great fellow was twisting it like a willow twig.

"Hello," cried Hans, "what are you doing there?"

The man replied, "I chopped some firewood yesterday and now I'm twisting a rope to tie it up."

Excellent, thought Hans, *how strong he is*. He called to him, "Leave that alone, and come with me." The fellow came down. He was a whole head taller than Hans, and Hans was not little. "Your name is now Fir Twister," said Hans.

They went on together until they heard something knocking and hammering with such force that the ground shook at every stroke. A giant was striking great pieces off a mighty rock with his fist. When Hans asked what he was doing, he answered, "At night, bears, wolves and other vermin come and snuffle about me and won't let me rest, so I want to build myself a house with these rocks."

Hans thought, *I can make use of this one also*. He said, "Leave your house building, and come with me. You shall be called Rock Splitter." The man consented, and all three strong men roamed through the forest. Wherever they went, the wild beasts were terrified.

One evening, they came to an old deserted castle, and they slept in the great hall. They arranged that each day, taking turns, two of them would go out hunting, and one would stay at home and cook their meat.

Fir Twister stayed at home the next day; Hans and Rock Splitter went out hunting. When Fir Twister was busy cooking, a shrivelled-up little man came to him in the castle, and asked for some meat. "Be off, you sneaking imp!" he answered. "You need no meat." To his astonishment the shrivelled-up dwarf sprang at him, and hit at him so vigorously that he could not defend himself, but fell on the ground and gasped for breath. The violent little man kept beating Fir Twister until he had thoroughly vented his anger.

When the two others came home from hunting, humiliated Fir Twister said nothing to them, thinking, *Let's see how they get on with the imp when they stay at home.* The next day Rock Splitter stayed home to cook, and he fared just as Fir Twister had done, being very ill treated by the dwarf because he didn't give him any meat. When the others came home in the evening, Fir Twister saw clearly what Rock Splitter had suffered, but neither said anything. They were thinking, *Hans must also have his share of this.*

Hans stayed home the next day, and did his work in the kitchen. As he was standing skimming the pan, the little old man came and without introduction demanded a piece of meat. Hans thought, *He is a poor wretch, I will give him some of my share, then the others will still have theirs*, and

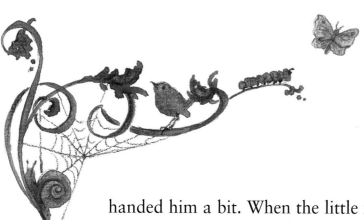

handed him a bit. When the little man had devoured it, he again asked for some meat, and good-natured Hans gave it to him, telling him it was a handsome piece, and that he was to be content with it. But the dwarf ate it and then begged again a third time. "You are shameless," said Hans, and gave him nothing. Then the malicious dwarf wanted to spring on him and beat him as he had beaten Fir Twister and Rock Splitter, but he had chosen the wrong man. Hans, without exerting himself much, gave the little dwarf a couple of blows which made him jump down the castle steps. Hans was about to run after him, but fell flat on his face. By the time he stood up again, the little man had got away from him. Hans hurried after, into the forest, and saw him slip into a hole in the rock. Hans went home, but he had marked the spot.

When the two other strong men came back from hunting, they were surprised that Hans was so well. He told them what had happened, and then they no longer concealed what had happened on their days at home. Hans laughed and said, "It served you quite right. Why were you so mean with your meat? It is a disgrace that you who are so big should have let yourselves be beaten by that little imp of a man."

Then they took a basket and a rope, and went to the hole in the rock where the little man had run, and let Hans down in the basket, holding his club.

When Hans reached the bottom, he found a door, and when he opened it, a girl was sitting there who was so beautiful that no words could express it. By her side sat the shrivelled little man who grinned at Hans like a cat. The girl was bound with chains, and looked so mournful that Hans felt great pity for her and was determined to help her escape. He swung his club, giving the wicked little man such a blow that he fell down dead. Immediately the girl's chains fell away, and Hans was enraptured with her beauty. She told him she was a King's daughter. A savage count had stolen her away from her home and imprisoned her there among the rocks, because she would not speak to him. The count had set the dwarf as a watchman, and she had suffered terrible misery.

Hans placed the girl in the basket and had her drawn up. The basket came down again, but Hans did not trust his two companions, thinking, *They have already shown themselves to be false, and told me nothing about the shrivelled little man. Who knows what design they may have against me.* So he put his club in the basket instead of getting in himself, and it was lucky he did, for when the basket was halfway up, they let it fall again. If Hans had been in it he would have been killed.

Now he did not know how he was going to get out of the hole in the rock, and turning it over repeatedly in his mind he could not come up with an answer. *It is indeed sad,* said he to himself, *that I will have to waste away down here.* But as he was walking about despairing, he wandered into the chamber where the girl had been sitting, and saw that the dead little man had a ring on his finger that shone and sparkled. He pulled it off and placed it on his own finger, then when he turned it round, he suddenly heard something rustle above his head. He looked up and saw spirits of the air hovering over him. They told him he was their master, and asked what they could do for him. Hans was at first struck dumb, but then, recovering his wits, asked them to carry him up out of the rock hole. They obeyed instantly, and it felt just as if he had flown up.

When Hans emerged back into the open air of the forest, though, he found no one in sight. Fir Twister and Rock Splitter had hurried away, and taken the beautiful girl with them. Hans turned the ring, and the spirits of the air came and told him that the two men and the girl were on the sea. Hans ran to the shore, and there, far, far out on the water, he could see a little boat in which his disloyal friends were sitting.

In fierce anger, without thinking about what he was doing, he leapt, club in hand, into the water, and began to swim. But the club, which weighed a hundred tons, dragged him deeper, until he was nearly drowned. In the nick of time he turned his ring, and the spirits of the air came and bore him as swift as lightning into the boat. He swung his club and gave his wicked comrades what they deserved, throwing them into the water. Then he sailed with the beautiful girl, who had been very frightened, and who he had now saved twice, home to her father and mother. He married her, and all rejoiced greatly.

28

The House in the Forest

Apoor woodcutter lived with his wife and three daughters in a little hut on the edge of a lonely forest. One morning as he was about to go to his work, he said to his wife, "Tell our eldest daughter to bring my dinner to me in the forest, for if I come home for it in the middle of the day, I shall never get my work done. So that she cannot get lost," he added, "I will take a bag of millet with me and strew the seeds along the path for her to follow."

When the sun was high in the sky, the eldest daughter set out on her way with a bowl of soup, but the field sparrows and wood sparrows, larks and finches, blackbirds and siskins had pecked up the millet seeds hours before, and the girl could not find the track. Trusting to chance, she went on and on, until the sun sank and night began to fall. The trees rustled in the darkness, the owls hooted, and she began to be afraid. In the distance she saw a light glimmering between the trees.

Perhaps there are people living there, who can take me in for the night, she thought, and walked towards the light, which turned out to be coming from a house. She knocked at the door, and a rough voice called, "Come in."

She found an old man sitting at a table. His long white beard fell across the table and almost down to the ground. By the stove lay a hen, a cockerel and a brindled cow. The girl asked for shelter for the night. The man said,

> My pretty hen,
> My pretty cockerel,
> My pretty brindled cow,
> What do you say now?

"Duks," answered the animals, and that must have meant "yes", for the old man said to the girl, "Here you may have shelter and food. Go to the fire, and cook us our supper."

The girl found plenty of food in the kitchen and cooked a good supper for herself and the old man, but she didn't think of the animals. She ate, and when she'd had enough, she said, "Now I am tired. Where is there a bed I can sleep in?"

The animals replied,

> You have eaten with him,
> You have drunk with him,
> You have had no thought for us,
> So you can find out for yourself
> Where you can pass the night.

The old man said, "Just go upstairs, and you will find a bed." The girl went up, and went to sleep. The old man went up a bit later, and opened a trapdoor that dropped her down into the cellar.

When the woodcutter came home, he reproached his wife for leaving him hungry all day. "It is not my fault," his wife replied, "our eldest daughter went out with your dinner.

She must have gotten lost, but I'm sure she will come back tomorrow."

So the woodcutter asked for his second daughter to bring his dinner to him in the forest the next day. "I will take a bag of lentils and strew them on the path," he said. "They are larger than millet seeds so the girl will see them better and won't lose her way."

At dinner time the second daughter carried the food out into the forest but the lentils on the path had disappeared. The birds had pecked them up just as they had done with the millet the day before. The girl wandered in the forest until night, and then she too reached the house of the old man, where she asked for food and a bed. The old man asked the animals,

My pretty hen,
My pretty cockerel,
My pretty brindled cow,
What do you say now?

The animals again replied "Duks," and everything happened just as it had happened the day before. The girl cooked a good meal, ate and drank with the old man but did not think of the animals, and when she inquired about her bed they answered,

You have eaten with him,
You have drunk with him,
You have had no thought for us,
So you can find out for yourself
Where you can pass the night.

When she was asleep the old man came, looked at her, shook his head, and dropped her down into the cellar.

On the third morning the woodcutter said to his wife, "Send our youngest child out with my dinner today. She has always been good and obedient, and will stay on the right path instead of roving about like her sisters, the wild bumblebees."

The mother did not want to send her dear third child in case she became lost like the older two, but the father said he would strew some peas on the path, because peas are even larger than lentils, and they would show the girl the way.

By the time the youngest daughter went out with her basket on her arm, the wood pigeons had pecked up all the peas, and she did not know which way to turn. She was full of sorrow, thinking all the time of how hungry her father would be, and how sad her good mother would be if she could not find her way home.

At length, when it grew dark, she saw the light and came to the house in the forest. She asked to spend the night there, and the man with the long beard again asked his animals,

My pretty hen,
My pretty cockerel,
My pretty brindled cow,
What do you say now?

"Duks," they replied. Then the girl went and petted the cockerel and hen, stroking their smooth feathers with her hand, and she caressed the brindled cow between her horns.

When she had made some good soup, she said, "Aren't the good animals having something? Outside there is plenty of food. I will look after them before I have my own supper." She stewed barley for the cockerel and hen, and brought in an armful of sweet-smelling hay for the cow. Then she fetched a bucketful of water in case they were thirsty.

When the animals were fed, the girl sat at the table by the old man, and ate her soup. Then she asked where she could go to bed. The animals replied,

> You have eaten with us,
> You have drunk with us,
> You have had kind thought for all of us,
> We wish you goodnight.

She went upstairs, said her prayers and fell asleep.

She slept quietly till midnight, but then was woken by the sound of cracking and splitting in every corner of the house. The doors sprang open, and beat against the walls, the beams groaned as if they were being torn out of their joints, it seemed as if the staircase was falling down, and there was a crash as if the entire roof had fallen in. But when all grew quiet once more, the girl realised she was not hurt, and she fell asleep again.

When she woke in the morning with the brilliant sunshine, what did she see? She was lying in a vast hall, and everything around her shone with royal splendour: golden flowers woven in silk tapestry hung on the walls, her bed was made of ivory with a canopy of red velvet, and on a chair close by was a pair of slippers embroidered with pearls. The girl thought she must still be dreaming, but three richly clothed servants came in and asked what they could do for her.

She replied, "Where is the old man? I will get up at once and make some soup for him, and then I will feed the pretty hen, and the pretty cockerel, and the pretty brindled cow."

But instead of the old man with the long beard, a young, handsome man came to her. He said, "I am a King's son. I was bewitched by a wicked witch, and made to live in this forest as an old bearded man. No one was allowed to be with me but my three servants in the form of a hen, a cockerel and a brindled cow. The spell could not be broken until a girl came to us whose heart was so good that she showed herself full of love, not only towards other people, but also towards animals. You have done this. At midnight we were set free, and the old hut in the forest changed back again into my royal palace."

The King's son ordered the three servants to bring the girl's father and mother to the palace for the marriage feast. "But where are my two sisters?" asked the girl.

The King's son replied, "I have locked them in the cellar, but tomorrow they will go and live as servants on a farm beyond the forest, where they will learn to be kind and not to leave poor animals hungry."

29

The Shoemaker and the Elves

Ashoemaker, by no fault of his own, had become so poor that at last he had nothing left but the leather to make one pair of shoes. In the evening, he cut out the shoes he would sew the next morning, lay down quietly in his bed, said his prayers and fell asleep.

The next morning, he was about to sit down to work when he found the two shoes standing finished on his table. He was astounded, and did not know what this could mean. He took the shoes in his hands to examine them. They were so neatly made that there was not one bad stitch in them; they were crafted like a masterpiece.

Soon after, a customer came in, who was delighted with the beautifully made shoes and paid extra for them. With this money, the shoemaker was able to buy leather for two more pairs of shoes. He cut them out at night, and the next morning he was about to set to work on them with fresh hope, but discovered they had already been made. Buyers came for these shoes, and from them he received enough money to buy leather for four more pairs. The following morning, he found the four pairs made, and so it went on. What he cut out in the evening was finished by the morning, and done with such skill that customers loved them. The shoemaker was no longer poor, and at last became a wealthy man.

One evening, not long before Christmas, the man said to his wife before going to bed, "What do you think: shall we stay up tonight to see who it is that gives us this helping hand?" The woman liked the idea, so they lit a candle, hid themselves in a corner of the room and watched. When it was midnight, three little men with ragged clothes came, sat down at the shoemaker's table, and took all the leather that was cut out before them. They began to stitch and sew and hammer so precisely and so quickly with their little fingers that the shoemaker could not take his eyes off them. The little men did not stop until all the shoes were made, and then they ran quickly away.

Next morning, the shoemaker's wife said, "The little men have made us rich. We must show that we are grateful for it. Their clothes are ragged and they must be cold. I will make them little shirts and coats and vests and trousers, and knit each of them a pair of stockings, and you could make them three little pairs of shoes."

The man said, "I would be very glad to do that."

A few nights later, when everything was ready, instead of the cut-out leather for making into shoes, they laid their presents all together on the table, and then hid to watch what would happen. At midnight, the little men came bounding in, ready to get to work. They did not find any cut-out leather to work on, but only the handsome little clothes. At first they were astonished, and then they were delighted. They dressed themselves in the shirts and coats and vests and trousers and stockings and shoes with great speed, singing,

> Now we are boys so fine to see,
> We need no longer cobblers be!

They danced and skipped and leapt over chairs and benches. Then they danced out the door. They never came back, but all went well for the shoemaker, and his business flourished through all the days of his life.

〜 30 〜

The Goose Girl at the Well

Once upon a time there was a very old woman, who lived with her flock of geese in a remote clearing among the mountains. She had a little house in the clearing, which was surrounded by a large forest. Every morning the old woman hobbled among the trees collecting grass for her geese and picking wild fruit. She carried everything she gathered on her back. Anyone watching would have thought that the heavy load must have weighed such an old, bent woman to the ground, but she never failed to bring her burden home.

She was always courteous, but local people avoided meeting her if they could help it, taking a roundabout way as they walked through the forest. When a father and his sons passed her, he would whisper to them, "Beware of that old woman. She has claws beneath her gloves: she's a witch!"

One morning, a handsome young man was travelling through the forest. The sun shone bright, the birds sang, a cool breeze crept through the leaves, and he was full of joy and gladness. He saw the old woman kneeling on the ground cutting grass with a sickle. She had already thrust a whole load into her cloth, and near it stood two baskets filled with wild apples and pears. "But, good woman," said he, "how will you carry all that?"

"I must carry it, dear sir," she answered. "Rich folk's children have no need to do such things, but with peasant folk the saying goes 'don't look behind you, you will only see how crooked your back is!'" He remained standing by her, and she asked him to help her with the load. "You still have a straight back and young legs; it would be a trifle to you. Besides, my house is not far from here, it stands behind the hill. How soon you would bound up there!"

The young man took compassion on the old woman. "My father is not a peasant," replied he, "but a rich count; nevertheless, so that you may know it is not only peasants who can carry things, I will take your bundle."

"If you will try it," she said, "I shall be very glad. You will certainly have to walk for an hour, but what will that matter to you? And you will carry the apples and pears as well?" An hour's walk seemed a little more serious to the young man, but the old woman would not let him reconsider. She packed the bundle on his back, and hung the two baskets on his arm.

"See, it is quite light," she said.

"No, it is not light," answered the count, and pulled a rueful face. "In truth, the bundle weighs as if it were full of cobble stones, and the apples and pears are as heavy as lead! I can scarcely breathe." He had a mind to put everything down again, but the old woman would not allow it.

"Just look," said she mockingly, "the young gentleman will not carry what I, an old woman, have so often dragged along. You are ready with fine words, but when it comes to action, you want to take to your heels." While he walked on level ground, the load was still bearable, but when they came to the hill and had to climb, and the stones rolled down under his feet as if they were alive, it was beyond his strength.

"I can go no further," he said, "I want to rest a little."

"Not here," answered the old woman. "When we have arrived at our journey's end, you can rest, but now you must go forward. Who knows what good it will do you?"

"Old woman, you are becoming shameless!" said the count, and tried to throw off the bundle, but it stuck fast to his back as if it grew there. He turned and twisted, but he could not get rid of it. The old woman laughed at this, and sprang about quite delighted.

"Don't get angry, dear sir," said she, "you are growing as red in the face as a turkey! Carry your bundle patiently. I will give you a good present when we get home."

What could he do? He was obliged to submit and crawl along patiently behind the old woman. She seemed to grow more and more nimble, and his burden still heavier. All at once she jumped up onto the bundle. The youth's knees trembled, but when he did not go on, the old woman hit him on the legs with stinging nettles. Groaning continually, he climbed the mountain, reaching the old woman's house just as he was about to drop.

When the geese saw the old woman, they flapped their wings, stretched out their necks and ran to meet her, cackling. Behind the flock walked a servant woman, strong and big, but ugly as night. "Hello, good Mother," she said to the old woman.

"Hello, my dear daughter," she answered. "I have met this kind gentleman, who has carried my burden for me.

He even carried me on his back when I was tired. The way, through, has not seemed long to us; we have been merry, and have been cracking jokes with each other all the time."

At last the old woman slid down, took the bundle off the young man's back, and the baskets from his arm, looked at him quite kindly, and said, "Now seat yourself on the bench by the door, and rest. You have fairly earned your wages, and they shall not be wanting." Then she said to the goose girl, "Go into the house, my dear daughter; it is not right for you to be alone with a young gentleman, he might fall in love with you."

The count didn't know whether to laugh or to cry. *Such a sweetheart as that*, thought he, *could not touch my heart.*

The old woman stroked her geese as if they were children and then went into the house with her daughter. The youth lay down on the bench, under a wild apple tree. The air was warm and mild. Across the clearing stretched a green meadow, which was dotted with cowslips, wild thyme, and a thousand other flowers. Through it rippled a clear brook on which the sun sparkled, and the white geese went walking backwards and forwards, or paddled in the water. "It is quite delightful here," said he, "but I am so tired that I cannot keep my eyes open; I will sleep a little. I only hope a gust of wind does not come and blow my legs off my body, for they are as rotten as old sticks."

When he had slept a little while, the old woman came and shook him awake. "I have certainly treated you badly," said she. "Still, you will live. You have no need of money and land, so here is something else for you." She thrust a green crystal box into his hand, cut from a single emerald. "Take great care of it," said she, "it will bring you good fortune."

The count sprang up, feeling quite recovered. He thanked the old woman for her present, and set off without once looking back at her or her daughter.

He wandered in the mountains and forest for three days before he reached a large town. As no one knew him, he was led into the royal palace, where the King and Queen were sitting on their thrones. The count fell on one knee, drew the emerald box out of his pocket, and laid it at the Queen's feet. Hardly had she opened it and looked inside, than she fell down, as if dead. The count was seized by the King's servants and was being led to prison, when the Queen revived, and ordered them to release him. She said she wished to speak with him in private.

When the Queen was alone, she began to weep bitterly, and said, "Of what use to me are the splendours and

honours with which I am surrounded? Every morning I wake in pain and sorrow.

"I had three daughters. The youngest was so beautiful that the whole world looked on her as a wonder. Her skin was as white as snow, her cheeks as rosy as appleblossom, and her hair as radiant as sunbeams. When she cried, pearls and jewels fell from her eyes instead of tears. When she was fifteen years old, the King summoned all three sisters to come before his throne. You should have seen how all the people gazed when the youngest entered, it was just as if the sun were rising! Then the King said, 'My daughters, I know not when my last day may come; today I will decide what each of you will receive at my death. You all love me, but the one of you who loves me best, shall receive the most.'

"Each of them said she loved him best. 'Can you not express,' said the King, 'how much you love me?' The eldest spoke. 'I love my father as dearly as the sweetest sugar.' The second, 'I love my father as dearly as my prettiest dress.' But the youngest was silent. Their father said, 'And you, dearest child, how much do you love me?' 'I cannot find a comparison for my love,' she said. But her father insisted that she name something. At last she said, 'Even the best food cannot please me without salt, therefore I love my father like salt.'

"When the King heard that, he fell into an angry passion, and said, 'If you love me like salt, your love shall also be repaid with salt.' He divided his kingdom between the two older sisters, and ordered that a sack of salt be bound to the back of the youngest, and that she be taken into the wild forest. We all begged and prayed for her," said the Queen, "but the King's fury did not soften. How she cried when she had to leave us! The whole road was strewn with the pearls that flowed from her eyes. The King soon repented of his severity, and had the forest searched for the poor child, but no one could find her. When I think that the wild beasts have devoured her, I know not how to contain my sorrow. I hold on to the hope that she is still alive, and may have hidden herself in a cave, or found shelter with compassionate people.

"When I opened your little emerald box, a pearl lay inside exactly like those which used to fall from my daughter's eyes. You can imagine how the sight of it stirred my heart. You must tell me how you came by that pearl."

The count told her that he had received the box from an old woman in the forest, who had appeared very strange to him and must be a witch, but that he had neither seen nor heard anything of her daughter.

The King and the Queen resolved to seek out the old woman. Where the pearl had been, they hoped they would have news of their youngest child.

The old woman was sitting in that lonely clearing at her spinning wheel. It was dusk, and the geese were coming home from the pasture, uttering their hoarse cries. Soon afterwards, the servant daughter also entered. They both sat spinning for a while until they heard an owl cry "Oo-hoo!" three times. The old woman said, "Now, my little daughter, it is time for you to go out and do your work." The ugly daughter rose and went out over the meadows and into a valley. Eventually she came to a well. The moon had risen. The girl removed a skin that covered her face, then bent down to the well and began to wash herself. How she was changed! When the grey mask fell off, her golden hair broke forth like sunbeams. Her eyes shone out as brightly as the stars in heaven, and her cheeks bloomed a soft red like appleblossom.

But the beautiful girl was sad. She wept bitterly. One tear after another rolled through her long hair to the ground. There she sat, until startled by a crack in the boughs of a nearby tree. She sprang up like a deer hearing a gunshot, put on the old skin and sprinted away.

When she reached home, trembling, she found the old woman standing on the threshold. The servant daughter was about to relate what had happened, but the old woman laughed kindly, and said, "I already know everything. Do you not remember that it is three years today since you came to me? Your time is up; we must part."

The girl was terrified, "Alas! Where shall I go? I have no home to go to. Do not send me away!"

The old woman would not tell the girl what lay before her. "My stay here is over," she said to her, "and when I go, house and parlour must be clean, therefore we shall sweep. Do not worry: you will have a roof to shelter you, and I will give you reward for your work that will keep you content. Go upstairs, take the skin off your face, and put on the silken gown you wore when you first arrived. Then wait until I call you."

The King and Queen had travelled with the count to seek out the old woman in the wilderness. The count had strayed away from them in the wood at night, and continued the next day alone. When darkness came, he climbed a tree to look ahead for the right path. By the light of the moon he saw a figure coming down the mountain. He could see it was the goose girl, the servant daughter of the old woman. How astonished he was when she went to the well, took off the skin and washed herself, and her golden hair fell down and she was more beautiful than anyone he had ever seen in the whole world. He hardly dared to breathe, but stretched his head as far forward through the leaves as he dared, and stared at her.

He bent too far and the bough he stood on suddenly cracked. The beautiful girl slipped into the skin, sprang away and disappeared into the darkness. The count rushed after her. He met the King and Queen, and they all continued towards the old woman's little house. The count told them what wonderful things he had seen by the well, and they did not doubt that the girl was their lost daughter.

The geese were sitting all round the little house, sleeping. The King and Queen looked in at the window, and saw the old woman quietly spinning, nodding her head and never turning round. The room was perfectly clean. But they could not see their daughter. They gazed at all this for a long time.

At last they took heart, and knocked softly at the window. The old woman rose, and called out quite kindly, "Come in, you are expected." When they had entered the room, she said, "You might have spared yourself the long walk, if three years ago you had not unjustly driven away your child, who is so good and lovable. No harm has come to her: for three years she has had to tend the geese. With them she has learnt no evil, but has preserved her purity of heart. And you have been sufficiently punished by your misery." Then she went to the stairs and called, "Come out, my little daughter." The door opened, and the princess stepped out in her silken garments, with her golden hair and her shining eyes, and it was as if an angel from heaven had entered the room.

She went up to her father and mother, fell on their necks and kissed them, and they all wept for joy. The young count stood near them, and when she saw him she became

as red in the face as a moss rose, though she did not know why. The King said, "My dear child, I have given away my kingdom, what can I give you now?"

"She needs nothing," said the old woman. "I give her the tears that she has wept on your account; they are precious pearls, finer than those that are found in the sea, and worth more than your whole kingdom, and I give her my little house as payment for her work." When the old woman had said that, she disappeared from their sight. The walls rattled a little, and when the King and Queen looked round, the little house had transformed into a splendid palace. A royal table had been spread, and servants were running here and there.

The story keeps going, but my grandmother, who told it to me, had partly lost her memory, and had forgotten the rest. I shall always believe that the beautiful princess married the count, and that they remained together in the palace, and lived there in all happiness so long as God willed it.

Whether the snow-white geese, which were kept near the little house, were really young girls whom the old woman had taken under her protection, and whether they now received their human form again and stayed as handmaids to the young Queen, I do not exactly know, but I suspect it may be true.

This much is certain, that the old woman was no witch, as people thought, but a Wise Woman, who meant well. Very likely it was she who, at the princess's birth, gave her the gift of weeping pearls instead of tears. That does not happen these days, or else the poor would soon become rich.

Discover More Fairy Tale Collections

Add enchantment to any bookshelf!
Enjoy some of the world's best-loved fairy tales in these stunning gift editions complete with ribbon markers and atmospheric illustrations.

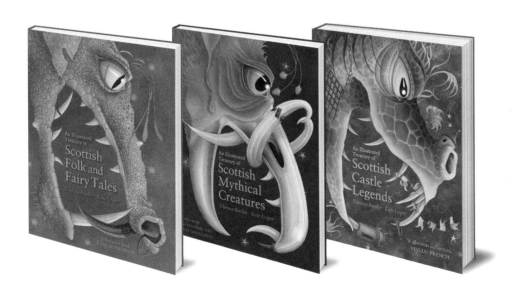

Floris Books